DANNY ORLIS

AND THE

MYSTERY OF THE WRECKED PLANE

DANNY ORLIS
AND THE
MYSTERY OF THE
WRECKED PLANE

BERNARD PALMER

ANEKO
PRESS

Please note that several books in the Danny
Orlis series are published by Sword of the Lord
Publications and are available for purchase on
their website, www.swordbooks.com.

Danny Orlis and the Mystery of the Wrecked Plane
© 2023 by Bernard Palmer
All rights reserved. First edition 1956.
Second edition 2023.

Scripture quotations from The Authorized (King James)
Version. Rights in the Authorized Version in the United
Kingdom are vested in the Crown. Reproduced by permission
of the Crown's patentee, Cambridge University Press.

Cover image: Adobe Firefly

Character illustrations: John Ball

Editors: Jon D. Fogdall

Aneko Press Youth

www.anekopress.com

Aneko Press, Life Sentence Publishing, and our logos are trademarks of
Life Sentence Publishing, Inc.
203 E. Birch Street
P.O. Box 652
Abbotsford, WI 54405

JUVENILE FICTION / Religious / Christian / Action & Adventure

Paperback ISBN: 978-1-62245-962-9

eBook ISBN: 978-1-62245-963-6

10 9 8 7 6 5 4 3 2

Available where books are sold

CONTENTS

CHAPTER 1

DANGER IN THE SKY

It was an early December morning in northern Minnesota, and the Lake of the Woods was sleeping beneath the shimmering whiteness of snow and ice. A few days before, a blizzard had whipped across the vastness of the Manitoba forests. It ignored the boundary between the United States and Canada, piling drifts about the Orlis buildings on the banks of Angle Inlet's Pine Creek and driving the mercury to the bottom of the thermometer.

But now the storm was over. The wind, as though to make up for its ugly display of violence, had lured the clouds away, giving the bleak, pale sun an opportunity to shine through the haze. There was little warmth in its slanting rays, but it brightened the spirits of those who had been devoting their time to digging out of the huge snow drifts. From across the frozen muskeg behind the Orlis cabins came the weirdly human cry of a lynx—and a ptarmigan, almost invisible against the white of the snow, hopped across a great drift in search of food.

Danny Orlis and his dad had scooped paths around the house and to the buildings they used regularly in the winter. A narrow lane ran around the house and back to the little building that housed the post office. It went on to the shed where the generator that furnished their electricity was sheltered, along with the snowmobiles and other equipment.

The cabins near the creek, which were used by fishermen and hunters, were almost buried in the snow piled high around the eaves. No one would think about using them until the spring thaws freed them from their silent white prisons.

Danny stepped out on the porch, a smile lighting his bright, young face. He was taller than the average fourteen-year-old and stockily built. His lean, well-muscled torso spoke eloquently of the vigorous outdoor life he lived.

His dog, Laddie, was half a step behind him—so close he could put down a mittened hand and touch Laddie's nose. That was the way it was with the broad tan and white collie. When Danny was in the house, Laddie was lying at his feet or curled up beside him on the floor near the wood heater. He watched while Danny did his homework and slept in his room at night. When his young master went outside, the dog was there, eager for a romp in the snow or a walk out on the ice to fish. Only when Danny got out the snowmobile did Laddie have to stay behind. He did so reluctantly, whining his protest.

That was the situation that particular morning. Danny dropped to one knee, pulled off his mitten, and ran his fingers through the dog's soft hair. "You can't go along this time, Fella," he said, as though Laddie could understand everything he said to him. "Mrs. Edgren called off school 'til Monday. So I'm going over to Matt Barton's on the Bearcat."

Laddie moved closer, pressing his head against Danny's hand.

"You have to stay home," his master repeated.

The big collie went with him out to the shed where the snowmobiles were kept. He stood by while Danny removed the cover, pushed one of the sleek, powerful machines out into the cold morning air, and pressed the starter. It groaned in protest against the cold that made it difficult to start, but after a few moments and several tries, the engine coughed and broke into a high-pitched whine.

Laddie would have followed Danny, but young Orlis stopped at the creek's edge, turned, and gestured toward the collie.

"Stay!" he shouted.

Laddie could not hear the command, but he understood the movement of Danny's hand and stopped, whining his disappointment.

Danny bounced across the snow and rough ice on the noisy machine, turned toward the mouth of Pine Creek, and headed for the house where Matt Barton lived with his grandmother. Matt heard the snowmobile when Danny was still half a mile away and came out to meet him.

"I wondered if you were going to make it today," Matt said. He was skinny as a poplar sapling and shorter than Danny Orlis by half a head. He had a shock of sandy hair and a scattering of freckles across the bridge of his nose. When he first came to the Angle, the freckles were scarcely visible, but now that he had been out in the sun, they had popped out like dandelions after a warm spring rain.

"We had some scooping to finish before I could leave."

"So'd I." He kicked the snow with his boot. "I'm glad Mrs. Edgren didn't have school today."

"Me too. I've been waiting all fall to go ice fishing."

Matt went back to the house and got his gear. "I forgot to tell you, I won't be able to stay very long," he said when he returned.

Danny hesitated before starting the engine once more. "How come?"

"Had a call from my mom on the radio the day before the blizzard hit," he said, excitement tightening his voice. "She's coming up to see me."

"Hey, that's neat!"

4

Matt acted as though he didn't know whether it was good or not. "She said she's got a surprise for me," he continued.

"Maybe it's a new snowmobile," Danny said, remembering how badly his friend wanted one of those machines for his own.

Matt hesitated. "I doubt that." The corners of his mouth twitched. "I know what I'd rather have than a snowmobile, but I don't suppose I'll *ever* get it."

Danny started the snowmobile and got on. Matt crawled on behind him and circled his waist with his arms.

"What's that?"

"Having her and Dad get back together again."

Danny opened the throttle, and they roared away in the direction of Little McCoy Island. He might have known that was what Matt was thinking about. Ever since he came to the Angle to stay with his grandmother, thoughts of his parents' divorce were never far from his mind. He was always talking about it. Somehow, he had the idea that it was his fault that his folks had separated. More than once he told Danny that he hadn't been able to figure out what he had done to cause the trouble.

"You can't be blamed for that," Danny said. "It's not your fault they weren't able to get along."

But Matt had not been able to accept his own lack of responsibility for the trouble between his parents. "They used to fight about me half the time," he continued. "If Mom said I could go down to the Arcade and play PacMan, Dad said it was a waste of money and I had to stay home. If he said I could go bowling or roller skating, she insisted that I stay in my room and do my homework." He breathed heavily. "I couldn't do *anything* to please them. If it hadn't been for me, they wouldn't have fought so much. They might even be together now."

Danny's folks didn't even argue that he knew of, so he hadn't had any experience with the sort of problem that faced his friend. Still, he was convinced that Matt's folks fought about other things first, and he just got caught in the middle. He tried to convince his friend of that, but Matt would not accept it.

"Grandma talks the way you do," he countered, "but I know why. It's just to keep me from feeling bad. I *know* who caused all the trouble between them. *Me!*"

They reached Little McCoy, and Danny went to the lee of the small, rocky island so the trees would shield them from the wind. He shut off the Bearcat. For an instant, the silence was deafening, and both boys glanced uneasily about, as though something was wrong.

"I've never fished this way before," Matt said, breaking the hush that enveloped them. "You'll have to show me how."

"There's nothing to it."

Danny got out the ice chisel and had Matt cut four holes through the thick ice a short distance apart. While his friend was doing that, he broke out their fishing tackle and rigged the tip-ups.

"Now, what do we do?" Matt asked, joining him. "What do we use for bait?"

"I have some night crawlers in my gear," Danny said. "In that little insulated box that keeps them from freezing."

In a few moments, the hooks were baited, and the boys moved to shore, where they built a small fire to warm themselves. They hadn't been there long when one of the tip-ups began to tremble.

"Hey, look!" Matt cried, jumping to his feet. "We're getting a bite!"

An instant later, the flag went up and he raced over to lift out a plump walleye about twenty inches long. "How about that!" he exclaimed, holding the fish high for Danny to admire. "Far out!"

"I had a hunch this was going to be a good day."

Matt rebaited the hook and reset the tip-up before returning to the fire. Silently, he sat down and warmed his hands. It was several minutes before he spoke again.

"I always wanted Dad to go fishing with me," he said, suddenly serious, "but he never had time. He was always working or at the bar with the guys."

Danny Orlis did not reply. He didn't know what to say.

They caught two more fish in the next half hour, and Danny roasted the biggest over the fire. Matt said it was the best he had ever eaten, and Danny had to agree with him. There was something special about a warm meal when they were out in the cold, particularly something they had caught and fixed themselves.

They had just finished eating when a low, monotonous hum pierced the quietness around them. Danny jumped to his feet, and, shielding his eyes with his hand, tried to spot the approaching aircraft. There were many planes in the Lake of the Woods country, especially small ones like Rankin's Cessna 180 that flew for Mr. Orlis, bringing in fishermen, hunters, mail, and supplies. Yet Danny was always excited and stopped whatever he was doing so he could watch as long as they were in sight.

That morning Matt did the same.

"Maybe that's Mr. Rankin bringing in your Mom," Danny told him.

Matt's lean figure tensed. "It might be, at that. But it wouldn't be Rankin bringing her," he said. "She was going to leave Denver the day before the storm. She would have gotten to Minneapolis that night. She would have rented a plane in the Twin Cities. But, if she left there this morning, she could be up here by now." Then he groaned aloud. "That's the pits! It's not her! The plane's heading for Kenora!"

"It looks more to me like he's going to our place or the Andersons' across the creek."

"Anyway," Matt continued, disappointment quieting his voice, "he's past Grandma's, so it can't be somebody bringing Mom in."

While they watched, the aircraft banked sharply and circled, losing altitude. As it came around, they saw that something was wrong.

"Look!" Matt cried.

One ski was securely in position, but the other dangled uselessly, the front end pointed up at a crazy angle. The pilot must have hit something on takeoff, shattering the bolts that held it in place.

"He can *never* land the way that ski is!"

Matt's eyes bugged wide. "Think he knows it?" Danny Orlis wasn't sure about that, but it was something they couldn't risk, though he didn't know what the pilot could do, even if he was aware of the problem. "If he comes close enough to see us, we've *got* to signal him!"

While they stared, the plane dropped lower and shifted its course slightly, so it was heading straight for them. "They're going to try to land."

Before Danny could answer, however, the engine coughed spasmodically and died.

"They'll crash! Come on!" Danny sped for the snowmobile and jumped straddle of it. His companion was half a step behind.

"What're we going to do?"

"Get over there so we can help them if we can!"

The pilot worked desperately in an effort to get the engine started. It backfired twice and almost took off, but then it died again. Danny started the snowmobile and threw it into gear. It lurched forward as the track bit into the snow, almost throwing Matt from his precarious perch behind him.

The aircraft was drifting lower now, gliding silently as an eagle, but without the grace of the big bird. Whoever was in the light craft knew about the broken ski. Even as the boys stared, the passenger's door opened and a man leaned out with a long, slender object in his hand. The aircraft was too far away for the boys to see what he was holding, but it was obvious to Danny what he was trying to do. He wanted to put the pole, or whatever it was, on the ski and push the sturdy slat down under the strut. It slipped off three times before he finally got it into place.

Now, if it would only stay!

"Dear God!" Danny prayed in silence, "help them to get down safely!"

CHAPTER 2

THE CRASH

The Bearcat increased in speed as Danny opened the throttle. The snowmobile hurtled over the rough ice in the direction the faltering aircraft was headed as it lost altitude. Matt tightened his grip on Danny's waist to keep from falling as they careened around the long pressure ridge and swayed danger- ously, coming back on course.

Danny prayed in silent desperation that God would spare the people in the aircraft from seri- ous injury. For a moment it seemed that his frantic prayer would be answered. The plane righted itself as the engine caught with a throaty roar and began to gain altitude.

"They're going to make it!" Matt cried hopefully in his companion's ear.

But that was not to be. The motor ran for the space of roughly twenty seconds or so, then it sputtered and cut out. Almost at the same instant, the craft disappeared behind the trees covering a long, narrow island. The boys stared helplessly at the place where the aircraft had floundered out of sight.

"They—" Danny's voice choked off, terror clutching the words in his throat as the awful, splintering crash echoed and re-echoed through the still, cold morning. The impact was so great that the wreckage hurtled crazily into the air just above the trees. It hit the ice again, a split second later, with a loud, rupturing blast followed by silence. A deathlike hush drove fear to the depths of Danny's heart. "They crashed!" he cried.

"W–what're we going to do now?" his companion demanded. He didn't want to approach the wrecked plane. "We–we'd better go back and get your dad, hadn't we?"

"Not yet! We've got to see if we can help those guys!"

"They won't need any help," Matt said numbly. "That's for sure."

Danny had to agree with him. He didn't see how anyone could survive a crash like that, but they couldn't risk leaving without finding out for sure. If anyone had survived, they would need help immediately. Cold as it was, they would freeze to death, even if they weren't killed by their injuries.

"We can't take a chance on it!" Danny told him, coaxing the last ounce of speed from their machine.

They sped toward the narrow island, whipped around the point, and saw the wreckage lying motionless on the snow and ice.

"They're all *dead*!" Matt exclaimed miserably.

Danny said nothing. He, too, was gripped by the icy fingers of dread as they rapidly approached the wreckage. One wing had been torn off the fuselage and lay fifty feet or so away. Half the tail assembly had crumpled, and the landing gear was gone, scattered along the final skid marks gouged deep in the ice.

Danny brought the snowmobile to a halt some distance from the aircraft.

"You aren't going over there!" Matt shouted as loudly as though the snowmobile were still hurtling at full throttle.

Danny hesitated, staring at the gasoline dripping from the ruptured lines. Fire could break out at any instant. But he couldn't let that stop him. He *had* to check the cabin to see if either of the two men was still alive!

"Stay here, Matt!" he ordered. "I'll be back in a sec!"

Slowly Matt got off the Bearcat and followed his friend. He was afraid—he wouldn't deny that. Gasoline could drip onto the hot engine or an exposed electrical connection or wiring, and the whole aircraft could burst into flames. If he had his way, they would be speeding across the lake to get Carl Orlis and some of the other men to examine the aircraft and get the men out. There was no doubt in his mind that the pilot and his passenger were dead. They were slumped grotesquely in the small cabin, blood frozen on their heavy parkas.

But Matt knew better than to argue with Danny when he had made up his mind that he should do something. He couldn't let him go alone, so he followed his friend to the wrecked plane. The door on the passenger's side had been wrenched open by the impact and hung from one hinge. A swarthy, hard-faced individual in a wolf-skin parka slumped in the seat, held in place by the seat belt.

"He's dead!" he shouted.

Matt glanced up at the dripping gasoline and saw a tiny wisp of smoke. "They're both dead! And this thing's going to blow up any second! Let's get out of here!"

Danny's heart ached, but he also saw the smoke and realized the certain danger of the situation.

"Let's go!" As he turned to run back to the snowmobile, he saw a briefcase on the floor at the feet of the dead passenger. With the smoke curling up around his hand and at the front of the plane where the engine lay, he snatched up the case and sped to the snowmobile.

Matt had scrambled into the driver's seat and started the engine. As Danny leaped on behind him, he opened the throttle and they sped away from the wreckage. They had been traveling only a few seconds when a great explosion swallowed the roar of the snowmobile. The wreckage had burst into flames and exploded.

"Man!" Matt exclaimed, staring back at the fiercely burning plane. "We got out of there just in time."

"The Lord protected us," Danny said, his voice thin and emotionless.

"The Lord didn't have anything to do with it!" his companion said. "I saw that smoke and said we had to split!"

"That explosion could have come a few seconds earlier," Danny told him. "If it had, both of us would've been killed. I figure God kept the fire and explosion from happening until we were out of the way."

Matt Borden fell silent. Danny was always talking about God and praying and stuff like that, but he didn't see that God had done that much for either of them. Danny still had his share of problems, and Matt knew that he did, too. He had even tried praying himself, after he got acquainted with Danny Orlis and his folks. He was going to find out if there was anything to that prayer business. So, he started asking God to bring his folks back together and make it so he could go back and live with them.

But nothing ever came of it. Once or twice, he got letters from his dad that sounded like he was willing to try it again, but his mom was something else. All she did when he tried talking to her about taking his dad back was to get mad.

And those dudes in the plane. God sure hadn't done much for them. He was positive Danny had prayed for their safety, though he hadn't prayed out loud. And what good had it done? They were both dead!

No, he hadn't seen anything to that prayer business, he told himself. Yet, he couldn't help thinking about Danny Orlis and his folks. He had never seen a family as happy and relaxed. Even when things were best at home, his folks and he had never enjoyed such happiness. Danny said it was because they were Christians. And if that was the reason, he wanted it for himself, and his mom and dad. Only he didn't think either of his parents would go for it. They had to have their own way about everything. And he didn't think a Christian could do that. At least Carl and Mary Orlis didn't. Grimly Matt tried to push thoughts about God and Jesus Christ and being Christian from his mind.

Danny's heart hammered fiercely against his ribs as he and Matt raced toward his folks' home on Pine Creek. He was still shaken by the airplane accident that had taken the lives of the two strangers. He was glad they had checked the plane and knew for certain that the men were dead. It would have been terrible if they hadn't gone over to look and the plane had exploded into flames. For the rest of their lives they would have wondered if they could have saved those men, had they gone to the aircraft right away.

He wished his dad had been there. Maybe he could have shut off the gas or something so the plane wouldn't have burned. But he and his companion had done the best they could. No one could do better than that.

The boys had been traveling twenty minutes or so when they saw two snowmobiles racing toward them at top speed.

"There's Dad and Mr. Anderson," Danny shouted over his shoulder. "They must've seen the plane crash and are coming out to find out if there's anything they can do."

He felt better just knowing that his dad and their neighbor were on their way.

A few minutes later they met. Carl Orlis and Mr. Anderson shut off their machines, and Danny and Matt glided up to them.

"We saw that plane go down. What happened, Danny?"

Hurriedly the boys told them everything they had seen—that there had been a loose ski on the passenger's side at first, and then the motor started to miss, causing the crash.

"Nobody could have survived that fire," Mr. Orlis said. "We could see it from the house."

"They didn't survive!" Danny said, shuddering.

Mr. Anderson turned to Mr. Orlis. "What do we do now, Carl?" he asked.

"We've got to get word to the authorities as quickly as we can," he said. Then he turned to Matt. "Have you got that ham radio of yours set up and working?"

"Sure have!" Matt's grin was wide. It would be good to use his radio for something other than having fun. Until now he used it to see how many different states and provinces of Canada he could contact and how many cards from different cities he could get.

"Would you go to your grandmother's and get in touch with someone who'll phone Sheriff Reddington at Roseau? Tell him he's needed at Angle Inlet as soon as he can get here."

"Should I tell him why?" Matt asked. "Should I tell him about the accident?"

"By all means."

Danny and Matt took off for Grandma Fuller's place, and Carl Orlis and his companion followed their tracks to the wreckage.

When the boys got there, Mrs. Fuller met them in the yard, concerned about the smoke she had seen. "I knew it wasn't a forest fire this time of year," she said. "The only thing I could think of was that something had happened to cause your snowmobile to blow up."

"Aw, Grandma," Matt said, "it wasn't anything like that." He told her about the plane wreckage and the two men who had been killed.

The boys went inside and took off their boots and parkas. "Come in with me, Danny," Matt said, starting for his bedroom. "I've been wanting to show you how my radio works. Dad got it for me for Christmas the year he stopped living at our house."

Matt sat down at the radio, turned it on, and gave his call letters. In a few minutes he had another ham operator who lived a few miles from Roseau in a small town Matt had never heard of.

"Hang in there, ol' Buddy," the stranger said. "I'll get Reddington on the phone."

By holding the telephone next to the speaker or the mike, as the situation required, the other operator made it possible for Matt to talk directly to the sheriff. He told him about the plane crash and that two men were killed.

"I'll be there as quickly as I can charter a plane," the sheriff said. "Over."

"Over and out."

Matt was about to switch off his radio when a ham from Baudette came on.

"I've been trying to raise you for more than an hour. Sounds like you've been having some excitement. Over."

"Enough to last for quite a while."

"I've got someone here who wants to talk to you." There was a pause, followed by a familiar voice. "Hello, Matthew, Darling."

"Mom!" In spite of himself, his lips trembled. "Where are you?"

"I'm here in Baudette, Silly. Where did you think I was?"

"We've been looking for you!"

"It's that silly snowstorm. I got to Minneapolis and couldn't get out because of the blizzard. But I'm coming now. We've got a plane chartered for tomorrow morning."

"We?" he echoed, uneasily. "Who's *we?*"

"I have a surprise for you."

He hesitated momentarily. The tone of her voice made him apprehensive. "There's only one surprise I want from you, Mom," he told her.

"Now, Matthew," she replied plaintively. "Please don't be difficult!"

CHAPTER 3

ALL THAT MONEY

Danny Orlis didn't want to stay at Grandma Fuller's any longer than he absolutely had to. He was anxious to get home as soon as possible in case the sheriff showed up earlier than expected. It wasn't every day a guy got a chance to get in on the investigation of a plane crash. He didn't intend to miss any of it unless he had to. But Matt's grandma insisted that he remain long enough to have some hot chocolate and cookies.

"When I saw you and Matt coming across the lake on that *machine* of yours," she said, "I figured you would be hungry, so I fixed something for you."

Danny could see that she would be disappointed if he didn't wait long enough to have lunch with Matt, so, reluctantly, he agreed.

They went into the kitchen and sat at the table while she poured steaming cups of hot chocolate from the kettle on the stove and got out a plate of freshly baked cookies.

As soon as the boys' cups were empty, she filled them again. "There's nothing like hot chocolate to warm you up," she said.

"That's for sure," Danny agreed. "Especially *your* hot chocolate. It's *super*!"

But Matt wasn't interested right then in what she was serving. He, too, was thinking about the sheriff coming back to the Orlis home and going out to the wreckage from there. Danny was going to get in on the investigation and he wasn't. He had to stay at his grandma's, where nothing exciting ever happened. Unless—the thought just came to him—he could talk his grandmother into letting him go back with his friend to spend the night. That would take some doing, he decided, but it was worth a try.

"Y'know, Grandma," he said when Danny was about to leave, "I think the sheriff is going to *need* me!"

Her eyes widened. "Whatever for?"

"I was an eyewitness. Danny and I saw the plane go down! At least we saw more of it than anyone else. And we were a lot closer. Sheriff Reddington is going to be awful mad if I'm not over there to help answer his questions."

"He can come and see you any time he wants," she informed him. "Danny or his folks will tell him where we live."

Matt didn't like that arrangement. It wasn't what he had in mind. "There's no need to put him to all that trouble. I could go home with Danny for the night and go to school from there tomorrow. I have to walk over there anyway, and it's going to be *awful* cold. You said yourself that you wished I didn't have to make that walk across the lake in the winter."

"That's right," young Orlis put in. "Matt can go home with me. That would make it easier for the sheriff. He'll be staying at our house tonight anyway. He could talk to Matt right there."

Amanda Fuller thought about that. "Are you sure it will be all right with your mom?" she asked uncertainly.

"Sure it will. He can sleep in my room."

"It would make it a lot easier for everybody," Matt added.

Relenting, she turned to her grandson. "You'll be sure and mind Mrs. Orlis, won't you?"

He promised that he would.

"And that you won't stay up half the night talking."

"We'll go to bed at our usual time."

"Mom'll see to that," Danny said.

"I suppose it will be all right for this *one* time," she said, "but I don't want you to make a habit of it."

Matt's grin was broad as he got into his boots and parka and went out to join his friend who was at the snowmobile by this time.

"Look, Danny," Matt said, pointing to the briefcase that was still on the big machine. "We should have given that to your dad when we saw him and Mr. Anderson."

"We can do that when we get home."

"Wonder what's in there?" Matt asked, climbing on the powerful machine behind his friend.

Danny had been thinking about that too. "We'd better let the sheriff open it."

"We can take a peak and he'll *never* know."

"That wouldn't be right," Danny said. "We both know that we shouldn't open it. Besides, the sheriff would blow his stack if we fooled around with that case on our own and he found out about it."

"That's just like the Fuzz!" Matt retorted, venom lacing his voice. "They're all gross!"

Danny was surprised at the anger his friend showed toward police.

"I don't think so," he countered, defending the authorities. "Sheriff Reddington has a job to do. I can't blame him for not wanting anyone to make it harder."

Matt Borden fell silent. Danny started the snowmobile, and they raced over the ice along the path his companion walked every morning. They reached the Orlis home an hour before the sheriff was flown in from Roseau. Danny took the briefcase to his dad.

"I pulled this out of the plane before we left," he said. "The passenger had it on the floor with his feet on it."

Mr. Orlis took the leather case, turning it thoughtfully in his hands. He noted that it was closed.

"You didn't try to open it, did you?"

Danny shook his head.

"Reddington will appreciate that. If you'd opened it, you might have destroyed some valuable evidence."

Carl took the briefcase to the front closet and set it behind the overshoes and boots.

Not long afterward, the plane bringing Sheriff Reddington to Angle Inlet flew in and landed on the ice in front of the Orlis home. He crawled out; a lean, hard-featured individual with piercing gray eyes that missed little going on around him. His steady gaze had a way of stabbing through the deceit and artful lying of those lawbreakers he brought to justice. Most knew better than to lie to him.

"I hated to call you out here, Dick," Carl said, "but I knew you had to be notified."

"It's my job," he said quietly.

"We saw the plane go down!" Matt broke in excitedly. "The ski on the passenger's side was loose, and the guy kept trying to get it in place under the strut so they could land on it. Then the engine started to miss and it quit…."

"We'll get your story later," Reddington said. "I'd like to fly out to the wreckage in time to get those bodies free and get them on their way to Roseau before dark." He turned to Mr. Orlis. "I'd like to have you come along and give us a hand, Carl."

Mr. Orlis nodded. "It's not the kind of job I like, but it's got to be done."

"Have you got a couple of neighbors who can come after us on snowmobiles?" That way the pilot won't have to land here on the way out."

"I can do better than that," Carl said. "The boys will come after us."

Danny glanced gratefully at his dad for including him and Matt. He wouldn't have had to do that. There were Mr. Anderson and Pete Reimer who lived behind them. They would have been glad to come out to the wrecked plane to pick them up. But that was the way his dad was. If he knew there was something Danny and one of his friends wanted to do, and doing it wouldn't cause any problems, he tried to help.

Dick Reddington hesitated, and the boys waited tensely. They were afraid the sheriff was going to say that they had better stay home. Then a grim smile broke his stern countenance, and they knew everything was going to be all right.

"I guess that'll work out OK. In fact, we might need their help. They might be able to help us piece together what happened."

The boys waited until the ski plane flew over on the way back to Roseau. Then they left Pine Creek on their snowmobiles and crossed the ice and snow to the place where the wreckage was lying. The sheriff and Mr. Orlis were looking over the section of wing that had broken off on impact. The rest of the plane, some distance away, was a twisted jumble of wreckage that had been burned almost beyond recognition. The prop was badly bent, and the engine was little more than a blackened chunk of iron.

"Did you find anything that would tell who the guys were?" Danny asked his dad.

Carl Orlis shook his head. "There are some numbers on the wing that should help to identify the plane," he said, "but any identification the men carried was destroyed by the fire. There doesn't seem to be anything that would tell us who the men were or what they were doing in this area."

Mr. Reddington came over to where they were standing. "I don't think there is any more we can do tonight," the sheriff said, disappointment in his voice. "I'll have to get in touch with the Federal Aviation Administration (FAA) in the morning. They'll inspect the wreckage to see if they can learn the cause of it. I'll check to see if the men filed a flight plan, and we'll find out who the plane is registered to." He breathed deeply. "Other than that, we're at a dead end. The plane's so badly burned we can't find out much of anything."

"What about the FAA?" Mr. Orlis wanted to know.

"They can do a lot more than I can. For one thing, they'll send in men who are experienced at unraveling things like this. I've handled only two other plane wrecks since I've been in office. I'm not expected to know much about them…." He turned back to the snowmobile, indicating that he was ready to leave. "Then, too, the FAA has the equipment to take tests of metal and plane parts that I've never heard of. I don't know what they can find out from a mess like this—if anything—but I can tell you this much, they'll give it a good try."

They returned to Angle Inlet where Mrs. Orlis had dinner waiting for them. Although the sheriff was not a Christian, as far as Danny knew, that did not stop Carl Orlis from having devotions that evening. Before anyone left the table, he opened the Bible and read a portion of Scripture. Then he asked if anyone had anything they felt they should pray about.

"We ought to pray for the families of the men who were killed in that plane this morning," Mary said.

"And that someone will be able to find out who they were," Danny added.

Thoughtfully his dad looked about the table, his gaze resting briefly on each one. "A tragedy like this," he began, "always makes me think of those who don't know Christ as their Savior. The men in that plane may or may not have been believers. If they were, they're in heaven with Christ tonight.

If they had never confessed their sin and put their trust in Him, they are lost eternally. That ought to be enough to make us think seriously about our own relationship with Him….

As they prayed, Matt thought about that. If he had been in that aircraft, he would have been one of those who was lost. He had never put his trust in Christ for salvation.

But he didn't have to worry about that, he told himself. He wasn't going to die yet. He was young. He had plenty of time.

When they finished their devotions, the sheriff pushed back from the table.

"Who got hold of me for you, Carl?" he asked.

"Matt, here." Mr. Orlis nodded in the boy's direction. "He's a ham radio operator."

"Fine." The sheriff glanced Matt's direction. "I've been wondering how I was going to get in touch with the people I've got to radio tomorrow morning. I'd like to do that before the plane comes in for me. It'll save time. We'll go over to your house in the morning before school."

It was then that Danny remembered the briefcase in the closet.

"Dad!" he said quickly. "There's something we've forgotten to give Sheriff Reddington."

The sheriff frowned darkly. "What's that?"

"Something I pulled out of the plane before it caught fire."

"That's right, Danny. So much has been happening I forgot all about it."

"Maybe you'd better let me in on this."

Danny went to the closet and got the briefcase. Sheriff Reddington set it on the table in front of him.

"It's locked!" he exclaimed. "Have you got a nail file, Mary? One of those that's cut away 'til it's real thin?"

She went to her bedroom and got two files. One was conventional and was too wide, but the other had been cut to a thin, curved point.

"This ought to do." He set to work. "The locks on these briefcases usually aren't too much."

In a moment he had it open on both sides. Laying the briefcase down, he tripped the latches and the case opened. He gasped audibly. The briefcase was filled with neat stacks of $100 bills.

"Man!" Danny said numbly. "Look at all that money!"

BAD NEWS FOR MATT

*S*heriff Reddington stared down at the briefcase filled with money. The color fled from his cheeks, and his features hardened. "I've been sheriff for twenty years," he said, "and I've never come across anything like this."

"What do you make of it, Dick?" Carl Orlis asked. As soon as he spoke, he knew he shouldn't have asked the officer such a question. The sheriff wasn't supposed to talk about cases he was investigating, but Carl couldn't help it. The words had slipped out.

"I wish I knew." Reddington straightened and looked up at his old friend. "But I can tell you this much. It isn't an ordinary accident. That's for sure. It's a matter that will have to be handled by federal authorities."

"You mean the FBI?" Matt blurted.

"Maybe. Maybe some other department." He was silent momentarily. "There is something I want to talk to you boys about," he said at last.

They eyed him, their faces taut with emotion. They were still stunned by the specter of all that money in the briefcase.

"I know it's going to be very hard for you not to tell anyone about this briefcase. Sometimes it's hard for me to keep quiet about the cases I'm working on. But it's very important. I want each of you to promise you won't say anything to anyone about the money or the briefcase."

The tone of his voice was disturbing.

"Not even Grandma?" Matt asked.

"Not even your grandmother. Will you give me your word that you won't say anything about it to anyone outside this room?"

The boys nodded solemnly.

The sheriff gave Carl Orlis a receipt showing he had turned over the briefcase and its contents to him, then took it into the bedroom where he would be staying. When he came back, Danny's dad suggested they play Tri-Ominos. The adults sat around the table and laid out the triangular pieces, face down.

"Danny," his mom said. "Don't you and Matt want to play?"

They shook their heads. How could they get interested in a game when their minds were racing?

Danny could still hear the aircraft crash into the ice. It was a sound he would never forget. And he could still see the wreckage scattered along the island, some distance offshore.

The next morning, as soon as it was light, Sheriff Reddington and Matt went over to his grandmother's by snowmobile. It took some time to raise a ham operator in the area at that hour of the day, and even longer to make contact with the FAA.

Reddington relayed the essential information tersely. A light plane on skis had crashed on the Northwest Angle of the Lake of the Woods when the engine malfunctioned. Both the pilot and his passenger were killed and burned beyond identification. The bodies had been sent to Roseau, Minnesota, where an attempt would be made to identify the victims.

The inspector on the phone was crisp and businesslike. A team of inspectors would be dispatched immediately. They should arrive sometime after noon.

Matt was surprised at how little information the sheriff had actually given to the FAA. They knew there was an accident and where it had taken place, but that was all. He supposed that was because of the money they had found and not wanting word of that to go out over the radio. Or, he decided, maybe that was just the way they did things. A thousand hams could have been listening to the exchange between the sheriff and the FAA. Some of them might be people the authorities didn't want to know about it. There would be plenty of time for the sheriff to give the rest of the information to the inspector in person.

Reddington thanked Matt and Amanda Fuller when he got off the radio and was putting on his heavy parka.

"Ready to go back now?" he asked the boy. "The plane's going to be in to pick me up before long. I don't want to keep the pilot waiting."

They went back to the Orlis home but didn't quite make it before the plane from Roseau arrived. They were half a mile away when the pilot landed and taxied slowly up to the big dock.

Carl came out and talked briefly with the sheriff before they took off, the briefcase on Reddington's lap. Matt didn't blame him for wanting to hang onto it so closely. If he and Danny had known what was in it, they would have handled it a lot differently themselves.

Danny's dad took Matt over to school on the snowmobile, getting him there an hour before lunch time. Mr. Orlis explained to the teacher why Matt was late, so he wouldn't get into trouble for it.

"I know," Mrs. Edgren said, smiling. "Danny told me about it earlier."

It seemed that Danny had told everyone else in school about seeing the plane crash and using Matt's radio to contact the sheriff and the FAA. As Matt went back to his seat, everyone in the room watched him enviously.

"How about that?" Don Clay, who sat behind him, whispered. "That must've been awesome!"

Matt nodded, swelling with pride at being the focus of attention.

"What'd the sheriff say?" Don continued. "Give us the inside dope."

He remained silent.

"Come on! You can trust me! We're friends!"

Matt saw that the teacher was busy correcting papers, so he risked turning in his seat and whispering softly. "He called the FAA. Or, rather, I got in touch with a ham operator in Minneapolis who got them on the line for us. They're coming out as quick as they can to have a look at the wreck."

Disappointment clouded his friend's face.

"That's all?" he asked.

"That's all."

"You've got to be kidding," he added suspiciously.

Mrs. Edgren looked up, frowning her displeasure, and Matt turned in his seat to face the front, his cheeks flushed.

At noon, as soon as the bell sounded, everyone went outside and crowded around Matt and Danny, demanding to hear the story of the plane crash again, in more detail. The boys didn't mind telling the story. It was fun to be the center of interest. But the kids weren't satisfied with what they said. They kept wanting to find out more. They believed that the sheriff must have shared some secrets with the two of them, and they weren't going to give up until they learned what those secrets were.

"What does he think made the plane go down?" one of the girls asked Danny.

"That's why the FAA inspectors are coming out. They'll try to find out what caused the crash."

"But doesn't Mr. Reddington have *any* idea why it went down?"

"If he does, he didn't tell us."

All the boys could think about was that briefcase filled with money, and they had given their word that they wouldn't say anything to anyone about it. Danny was afraid one of them might let it slip. And that would be terrible! He was thankful for the interruption when a plane came over at low altitude, waggling its wings.

"Think that's the FAA people?" Clay asked.

"Nope!" Matt's pulse quickened. "That's got to be my mom! She said she was flying in today."

Danny and Matt made their way back into the schoolhouse, sat in desks at the back of the schoolroom, and ate their lunch. Young Barton was so tense he could scarcely finish his meal. The bread was sawdust in his mouth, and the meat was tasteless as cardboard.

"Would you pray for me, Danny?" he asked hesitantly.

"Sure thing. What about?"

"I woke up early this morning thinking about Mom coming up to the Angle today. I decided I'm going to talk to her. When I see her, I'm going to ask her about going back with Dad so we can have a home like we used to."

Danny bowed his head and prayed silently. He asked God to work in the hearts of Matt Barton's mom and dad, that He would restore the love they had had for each other and would help them get their problems worked out so they would be willing to go back together again. Matt was watching Danny hopefully, and when his friend stopped praying, he relaxed slightly. He wasn't a Christian himself, but it was good to have Danny as his friend. He could pray for him.

Matt wished he could have left the schoolhouse right then and made his way back to his grandmother's so he could see his mom and talk to her. But he knew it wouldn't do any good to ask the teacher about taking the rest of the day off. She had already given them two extra days of vacation because of the blizzard. She wasn't about to let him out early so he could go and see his mom—even if he hadn't seen her for three months.

When classes were finally over for the day, the kids wanted to talk about the wrecked plane once more in an effort to get a few more shreds of information—things that were supposed to be secret. But Matt was in a hurry.

"We've already told you everything we can," he said, going out to Danny's Bearcat.

They followed him, still plying him with questions. As soon as young Orlis ran out of the building, his homework in a nylon bag on his back, they got on the machine, started the engine, and lurched away, gathering speed as they went. They bounced over the rough trail, past a couple of houses where some of their school friends lived, and approached the Orlis buildings from the back. Matt was about to ask Danny if he would take him on over to his grandmother's when they saw a plane wing slowly overhead, circle, and dip toward the frozen creek that fronted the house and fishermen's cabins.

"Looks like those men Mr. Reddington got in touch with are just arriving," Danny called over his shoulder. "Want to stop for a few minutes?"

Matt hesitated. He was torn between wanting to go in and at least see the inspectors who had come to examine the wreckage and his desire to get home as fast as possible.

If they had reached the house a little later, after the plane landed and the passengers were inside, he might have elected to go on without stopping. As it was, they arrived just as Carl Orlis grasped the wing of the sleek Cessna 180 and held it for the passengers to get out.

Danny stopped the snowmobile, and he and Matt hurried out to help tie down the new aircraft. While they were assisting the pilot, the two inspectors were introducing themselves to Carl and Mary Orlis.

"Sheriff Reddington told us that he had made arrangements for us to stay with you," Dr. Granville announced. "Is that right?"

"*We* don't have the nicest of rooms," Mary replied, "but you're welcome to stay with us, if you like."

"I'm sure they'll be fine."

They went inside and sat in front of the fireplace. The boys followed, trying to remain as unobtrusive as possible.

"We would like to rent a snowmobile with a sled to carry our equipment," Granville said. "And we would like to have someone take us to the wrecked plane." He paused thoughtfully. "Think that can be arranged?"

"I see no reason why it can't." Carl Orlis leaned back in the chair and crossed his legs. "I've agreed to help Anderson butcher a steer tomorrow," he said, "but it'll be Saturday, and Danny and Matt could go with you to see that you find the place."

Granville frowned. "They won't get us lost, will they?"

"No," Carl said, laughing. "They won't get you lost. Danny knows these woods and the lake as well as most men who've lived here for forty years, and Matt's not far behind him. They'll get you where you want to go all right."

"Besides," Danny put in, "we saw the plane go down and were the first to get there."

The inspector seemed unimpressed. "Fine. We'll leave at 9:00 in the morning."

With that they started talking about the blizzard and the National Hockey League. Granville was a fan of the Montreal Canadiens, while Carl Orlis followed the Wilds that made the Xcel Energy Center in Minneapolis their headquarters. They were still discussing the merits and shortcomings of their teams when Matt signaled Danny that he had to leave. Danny decided to take him home and left the house with him.

"Going to be able to go with us tomorrow morning?" Danny asked softly.

Matt shrugged. "If I'm not here by nine, go without me."

It was getting late by the time they neared Grandma Fuller's house. Danny knew it would be dark by the time he got back home, and he didn't much like to be out on the snowmobile at night. For that reason, he didn't shut off the Bearcat but stopped only long enough for Matt to dismount.

"See you tomorrow," Danny said.

The people in the house had heard the machine approaching and came out on the little front porch.

Danny's heart sank.

Matt's mom was there. He had never seen her before, but he recognized her from the pictures Matt showed him. A tall, dark-haired man about her age was standing with his arm about her waist. Danny had seen pictures of Matt's dad too. That wasn't *him* on the porch with her.

Matt saw it, too, and groaned aloud.

CHAPTER 5

WHAT CAUSED THE WRECK?

Matt stood by the snowmobile momentarily, staring at his mom and the man by her side. So that was the surprise she had for him! Somebody to take Dad's place! His stomach turned, and he felt a sharp, driving pain just above his belt. He wanted to climb on the snowmobile and go back home with Danny, but he couldn't do that. He had to go up to the house and meet his mom's newest friend.

He was glad to see his mom, of course. That was one of the things that caused him so much trouble. He loved her so much and wanted to get her and his dad back together so they could once more live as a family.

But no! Nothing ever seemed to work out right! It was no wonder Danny was a Christian. God had given him everything anyone could want, and more. He had a happy home with both his mom and dad there, loving each other and him. They didn't even quarrel and argue like a lot of people did. God had worked out all the things in Danny's life that really counted. He had reason to be a Christian.

But God doesn't care about me, Matt thought bitterly. He and Danny had been praying about this visit of his mom's ever since he knew she was coming. He had even worked out what he planned to say to her and had made himself believe that, somehow, he would be able to persuade her to come back and make a home for him and his dad. Now there was somebody else in her life. Maybe they were already married! And if they were, that would ruin everything!

Matt moved slowly toward the house, scuffing the snow with his boots. Dimly he heard Danny yell that he was leaving, and the snowmobile behind him started and gained speed as it sped away. Inside the gate he stopped. At that instant, his mom flew off the porch and dashed to him, throwing her arms about him.

"Oh, Matthew!" she cried tearfully. "I'm *so* glad to see you!"

Tears coursed down her cheeks.

"I've been waiting for *so* long!" she stammered. "I thought that blizzard would *never* end so we could get out of Minneapolis. Then we had to wait in Baudette to charter a plane to bring us up here." She laughed nervously. "And when we finally got here, you were in school. I wanted the pilot to land at the schoolhouse so we could see you there, but he wouldn't make two stops. We had to wait until now."

He knew he should say something, but if he did, he was afraid he would start to bawl, and he wasn't going to do that. Not in front of that stupid guy she had with her!

"Come on, Matthew." She took his hand and started forward. "I'm anxious to have you meet Robert."

His lithe, young body stiffened, and the muscles in his jaw grew hard, but his mom didn't seem to notice. She was too taken up with this guy who had come with her.

Her new friend—at least he supposed he was new—stood a full head taller than Matt's mom. He was an angular individual with lean features and gray eyes that seemed to bore into his gaze.

"Robert," she said nervously, "I want you to meet the *other* man in my life.... Matthew, this is Robert Osborne." Her smile flashed. "We're engaged to be married…. See!" She held out her new diamond ring for him to see. "It won't be long 'til I can take you home again!"

"Hello, Matt." Robert stepped forward and held out his hand.

Matt took it, hesitantly, and acknowledged the introduction. He was writhing inwardly. They weren't married, but they were engaged, and that was just about as bad. Now there was no use in talking to her! She would *never* agree to take Dad back! Something inside him died.

"I've got a boy about your age," Robert said, "but he's with my former wife right now, going to school."

And, Matt said angrily to himself, *I'll bet that son of yours feels the same as I do about you and Mom.*

"That's a nice snowmobile your friend has."

Matt nodded. "It's a Bearcat."

Mr. Osborne nodded. "I know. I bought one last year, myself, so Jason would have something to have fun with during the wintertime. When your mom and I get married I'll buy another one."

Matt cringed inside. Trying to buy his approval of the marriage wasn't going to work. He could tell him that right off.

"And in the summer, Jason has a three-wheeler. He uses it to tear all over my dad's farm in Colorado." Osborne laughed genially. "Sounds like I'll be stuck with another one.... You and Jason will have great times together. He's taller than you, but you remind me a lot of him."

Matt's expression did not change.

"Doesn't all that sound *wonderful*" his mom asked.

His frown deepened. "I–I guess so."

"I'm so anxious to have you meet Jason, I can hardly wait," she continued. "I wanted him to come along now, but Robert thought he had better stay in school."

Osborne saw that his bride-to-be was shivering in the cold. He put his arm about her protectively. "Don't you think we had better go in now, Marion, dear?"

She allowed him to guide her back to the house. Matt followed, staring at the snow covering his grandmother's small lawn. When they were inside and Matt had taken off his snowshoes and parka, his mom came over to him.

"Grandma said you've been as anxious to see me as I've been to see you."

He nodded.

"And you had something you wanted to talk to me about?"

His lips narrowed and begem to tremble.

"What good would that do?" he demanded. "Now?"

He turned abruptly and went into his room.

"Matthew!" she cried after him. "Don't be like that!"

Matt didn't sleep well that night. Every time he closed his eyes, he could see his mom and that Robert Osborne together. They were laughing and having a good time. He and his dad didn't mean anything to her anymore, he told himself. The only ones she seemed to care about were this new guy and his son Jason.

He got up and started to dress, though it was early and still dark, and the house was silent. But he didn't care. It gave him some time to be alone—to think. When the others came to the kitchen, he was staring morosely at the stove.

"I didn't expect to see you up so early," Osborne said, sitting across from Matt and pulling on his socks. "How about you and I going ice fishing this morning? That's something I've never done."

Matt's gaze was cold and expressionless. "Danny and I have something we've got to do this morning."

"I'm sorry about that," his mom's friend said. "I was counting on fishing with you."

"Grandma can tell you how," Matt said, "and you can go any place you feel like off the island."

Matt's mom came in just then and was disappointed that he had turned down the fishing trip with Mr. Osborne, but he insisted that he and Danny had to take the FAA inspectors out to the plane. He didn't *have* to go along, but he made it sound like he did.

He got to the Orlis house about the time Danny and the others were finishing breakfast. The boys filled the snowmobiles with gas and got them started so they were all ready to leave by the time Dr. Granville and his associate joined them. Danny and Matt rode one machine, and the two men, with the toboggan towed behind, rode the other.

They left the mouth of Pine Creek and angled across the ice and drifted snow toward the place where the aircraft wreckage was scattered grotesquely. In a few minutes they could see the parts of the plane lying there as though some giant had torn it apart with his hands and thrown it down.

"You boys can go back now, if you'd like," Granville said. "We can manage on our own from here."

"Oh, no!" Danny said quickly. "We'll stay—that is, if it's all right."

The chief inspector hesitated. "You'll have to keep out of the way," he said, "and be careful not to touch anything. We never know what is going to be the one piece that finishes the puzzle, so we have to take great care not to move anything."

They assured him that they would not touch any of the wreckage, whether they thought it was important or not.

"Fine." he said. "Just so we understand each other."

The men had apparently worked together for a number of years. Each knew what to do and what the other would be doing. They began at the forward end of the wreckage and painstakingly worked their way back.

At first Matt and Danny thought it exciting to be there watching the inspection, but after a couple of hours they realized it was slow and boring work—a meticulous examination of every piece of the damaged plane.

By noon, when they stopped for a sandwich and a cup of coffee, they had made what seemed to the boys slight progress. They had advanced only a short distance in the wreckage.

Every now and then they had taken off a part or a section of tubing, wrapped it carefully, and placed it on the toboggan. But they said nothing about the significance of the pieces they saved, and Danny and Matt didn't feel they could ask them.

"Tell us again how the plane acted when it lost altitude and finally disappeared from view," Granville wanted to know.

They told him everything just as they remembered it. It seemed strange to Danny that Granville would question them again. He would surely have

Sheriff Reddington's report—and Danny's and Matt's accounts were included.

He must have read the questions in Danny's eyes. "I know you gave your story to the sheriff," he said, "but I thought you might remember something that you had forgotten to tell him."

"What about the loose ski?" the other inspector put in. "Can you tell us anything about it?"

They both shook their heads. "Nothing we haven't told already. The plane looked as though it was headed directly for us. We thought maybe they were going to land. Then we saw that the ski on the passenger's side was loose at the front end and cocked in the air. The passenger had the door on his side open and was trying to hold a stick of some kind on the front of the ski to push it down into place. Then the motor acted up and it crashed." He gestured expressively.

"Have you seen that strut anywhere?" Dr. Granville asked suddenly. "The one the loose ski was fastened to?"

His associate got to his feet and went over to the plane. "The other one's here," he said after a few moments, "and both skis are here, but the strut is gone!"

Danny's eyes widened. "How could that be?"

"Was anyone else over here that you know of?" They shook their heads.

"Did you tell anyone exactly where the plane crashed?"

"Nope. Dad told us not to. He said you'd want to have everything the way it was when the accident happened."

The associate had remained at the wreckage, still looking around. "Here we are!" he exclaimed suddenly.

Dr. Granville and the boys leaped to their feet. "What is it?"

"I think I know what happened to that strut. Two guys came from the island and walked around the wreckage and back again."

"Are you sure?"

"Come and see for yourself."

The chief inspector led the way, and Danny and Matt followed. There was no mistaking it. Two men had come from the island and approached the wreckage. They must have gone around it, too, but the tracks close to the plane were so jumbled there would be no way of knowing who had been where. At any rate, the tracks indicated that the men had left the wreckage and had gone back to the island.

"Think they're the ones who took the strut?" Danny asked.

Dr. Granville shrugged. "Who can tell from the little evidence we have here? They might have been the culprits, or they might simply have been sightseers who came to take a look."

"But if they were," Danny said, "why would they have approached the wreck from the island side? Why didn't they come around on the ice?"

Dr. Granville bristled. "I'm an FAA inspector," he said coldly. "I don't do guessing or fortunetelling."

"Do you think those guys are still over there?" Matt asked, in spite of Danny's warning glance.

Dr. Granville surprised them both by answering. "Those tracks were made this morning. I'm sure of that. The edges are still crisp and sharp. But I wouldn't see any reason for anyone staying over there to watch us. To someone on the outside, this has to be about the most boring, unexciting job there ever was. I don't think *anybody* would hang around very long to watch us."

Nevertheless, Granville found a reason to send the boys home quite soon.

"Danny," he said, "I want you and Matt to take one of the snowmobiles and go back to the house. Tell your mom it looks as though we'll be staying for several days."

"I think she expects that," Danny told him. "I heard her and dad talking about it in the kitchen this morning."

The inspector's eyes narrowed. "Do as I say!" he grated. "And don't let me have to tell you again!"

Without arguing, Danny and Matt got on the snowmobile and left. Young Orlis drove to the end of the island and swung around to the other side.

"Where are we going now?" Matt demanded, shouting into the wind.

For answer, Danny closed the throttle, and the machine crept to a halt. "Don't shout so everybody can hear us!" he said tensely. "We're going around and see if there's any evidence of those dudes who walked up to the plane from the island."

"You think they might be over here?"

Danny shook his head. "I don't know about that. But I do know they didn't fly to the island. They had to get there somehow. I'd just like to see which direction they came from."

CHAPTER 6

"WE'RE GOING TO BE MARRIED"

Danny Orlis swung the Bearcat around the south end of the island and headed on a more westerly course. Matt tapped him on the shoulder after a minute or two and pointed in the direction of Pine Creek and the Orlis buildings. He nodded to signify that he understood but did not change his bearing.

Once again, his companion punched him in the shoulder. "You live that way!" Matt said. "Remember?"

"I know," Danny told him, "but there's something I want to see about before we go home."

Matt frowned. "Like what?" he asked suspiciously.

"Like whether there are snowmobile tracks headed for the wrecked plane."

Matt caught a tenseness in Danny's voice that hadn't been there before. "So, *you* think that strut was stolen!" he exclaimed.

"It's the only answer that makes sense. We already know that there was something wrong with it. Now it's gone! Why?"

Matt was silent for a moment. "There's only one reason anybody would swipe that piece from the wrecked plane that I can think of," he concluded.

"Right on! They wouldn't want Dr. Granville to find it, because they had done something to it to cause it to break."

"Like sawing it half in two!" Matt exclaimed, his eyes bright with excitement.

"That's probably the reason they sent us home," Danny went on. "They didn't want us to get mixed up in anything like that."

"That's the way I've got it figured. And it sounds smart. Let's you and me split!"

Danny opened the throttle enough to make further conversation difficult and continued in the direction they were going. Snow, fine as salt, was sifting down, and the gusty wind whipped it along the ice and over the drifts of the former storm.

It wouldn't be long until they would have to head back home, whether they succeeded in finding the telltale snowmobile track or not. He glanced at his watch. If it didn't start snowing harder than it was, he would continue on his present course for another ten minutes. If they hadn't located it in that length of time, they would have to give up for now. It wasn't worth the risk of getting caught in a storm. Besides, drifts would soon wipe out any track that was left. The snow and wind seemed to increase in intensity, and, with reluctance, Danny turned his machine about and headed for Pine Creek. Matt noted the change with approval.

For a time, the storm worsened, and Danny began to feel that he had made a mistake going out of his way in an effort to see if a snowmobile had headed toward the wrecked plane from the southwest. The storm might close in. Then Matt would have to stay with him that night. Which would be all right, of course, except that they wouldn't have any way of getting in touch with Matt's grandmother and his mom, and they would probably be terribly worried. Abandoning the search, he turned toward home.

As the boys neared the Orlis place, however, the snow let up unexpectedly, and the wind became little more than a whisper. The same dull, gray overcast reached from horizon to horizon, but a storm no longer seemed imminent. Danny had the impression that it had warmed up, but it probably hadn't.

"I think I'd better go on to Grandma's now, while I've got a chance," Matt said. "I don't *want* to, as long as Mom's there with—with *that* guy, Osborne. But I suppose I'll have to. She'll yell her head off if I don't."

Danny nodded. "We can swing over there now."

"I can walk."

"There's no need of that. We've got gas enough, and it'll take only a few minutes."

Danny Orlis pulled out of the creek mouth and headed for the island where Amanda Fuller lived. It was only a brief ride on the snowmobile, and he soon let Matt off near the front gate.

Robert Osborne was off somewhere when Matt got home, and Amanda Fuller was in the kitchen baking bread. His mom met him just inside the door. He saw that her features were taut with emotion, and there were dark circles under her eyes. She looked the way she used to when she and his dad had been fighting. His first thought was that she had quarreled with Osborne. Maybe they had had a fight and the plane came in and got him. That would be the best news he had had for a while, but he soon learned that was not the way it was.

"I asked Robert to watch for you," she began, her lower lip trembling, "and when he saw you coming, to go out the back door for a walk. I—I've *got* to talk to you, Matthew! *Alone!*"

The frown muscles in his face tightened.

"Can't it wait?" he asked curtly. "I'm hungry! Fact is, I'm about starved!"

"No," she retorted, "it can't wait! I've got to talk to you now!"

By this time, he had pulled off his heavy boots and was sitting on the chair inside the front door, staring insolently up at her. "OK. Shoot!"

"We'll go to your room, Matthew, so we won't be bothered."

Sarcasm curled his lips. "If we've got to go to *my* room, why'd you send that dude, Osborne, away?" For an instant she seemed flustered and unsure of herself. Her chin quivered, and there was a tremor in her voice when she spoke.

"I sent him away because—because—" She swallowed hard and jerked herself erect. "I did it because I did! That's why! And it's none of *your* business! I don't *have* to answer you!"

He followed her to his room and slumped in a chair, staring insolently at her. She pulled out a chair and sat across from him.

"Matthew," she began, tears filling her eyes. "I want some answers from you! Why don't you *like* Robert?"

He had been sure the little talk she wanted had to do with this Osborne dude, but he hadn't expected her to be so direct. It put him on the defensive.

"I just don't!" he snapped.

A tear escaped her eyelid and trickled down her cheek.

"You don't care whether I'm happy or not," she said. "All that matters to you is that no-good dad of yours!"

He swallowed against the lump in his throat.

"That's not true!" he blurted. "All I want is for us to be together again. *All three of us!*"

She got to her feet impulsively and went to the window, staring out at the trees. "I suppose *he* put you up to this!"

"Dad never put me up to anything! It's my own idea! Mine and Grandma's!"

Marion Barton turned to face him.

"I had a talk with *her* this morning, too! You all are so concerned about Craig Barton and yourselves!" She was on the verge of crying, but anger made her voice louder. "Nobody thinks about *me* and what *I* want! *I'm* the one whose life is ruined, but that doesn't matter! Just so the rest of you are happy!"

He stared numbly at the floor. He had worked out exactly what he was going to say when he talked to her, but now that the opportunity was here, he didn't know how to begin. It probably wouldn't do any good anyway, he told himself. She sounded as though she wouldn't listen to anybody—and especially to him.

Marion started to speak to her son but returned to the chair and sat down first.

"Matthew," she said finally, "I know how you feel about—about having your dad and me divorced, and I wish it could have ended differently than it did. When we got married, neither of us figured we would have trouble. But you don't know what it was like living with that man. He'd come home drunk and beat me and not give me any grocery money or pay our bills. It was terrible."

"And you'd get mad and run off for a week, leaving Dad and me alone."

She tried another tack. "Don't you understand? I have my own life to live. I'm entitled to *some* happiness. And Robert is the one who will give it to me! I know that now. You should get acquainted with him, Matthew. That's the reason he came up with me. So that you could learn to know and like him."

She reached out and took his hands in hers. Her grasp was cold as ice. "If you'd just give him a chance, you'd love him as much as I do. You'd forget all about that drunken dad of yours."

At that he jerked away from her, eyes blazing. "Don't talk about Dad that way!"

She started to cry, and it was a minute or more before she was able to speak.

"There's something else I've got to tell you, Matthew," she said.

"Go ahead. This seems to be jump-on-Matt-day."

"Don't be like that. Please!"

"OK, Mom!" he snorted. "I'm listening!"

"Have—have you been in any more trouble?"

The corners of his mouth tightened. "What do you mean, trouble?" he demanded, irritably.

"You know."

"With the Fuzz?" He laughed scornfully. "How could I get 'busted' up here? There aren't any pigs around."

"I—I was thinking about that other trouble," she said, faltering. "The one that caused us to send you up here."

"Pot?" he echoed. "How would I get a joint up here? Answer me that."

"I'm so afraid of dope, Matthew. Promise me you won't use it anymore—ever."

He didn't want to make a promise like that, because he didn't know what he would do if and when he went outside. But he knew she wouldn't stop hounding him until he said what she wanted him to say in a way that pleased her.

"If it means so much to you, Mom," he said. "I'll do it."

"Do what?"

"Promise that I'll never use pot or any other kind of dope again."

"On your word of honor?"

"On my word of honor."

That seemed to satisfy her, at least for the moment. She stood and touched the top of his head with the tips of her fingers.

"I have one other thing I haven't told you yet," she continued. "I am anxious to have you get to know Robert while we're here, because I have just told him that I will marry him as soon as the divorce is final."

The words slammed into him. He looked up at her helplessly.

She read the dismay in his eyes. "It isn't going to do any good to argue with me," she informed him. "My mind is made up."

Down the bay at the Orlis home, Danny was sitting before the fireplace, his fingers tangled in the shaggy hair at Laddie's neck. He had put a log on the dying embers a few minutes before, and the flames were licking around it and reaching upward. The smoke curled lazily toward the chimney.

Dr. Granville and his associate had come back a few minutes before. They had Carl Orlis place the items they brought from the wrecked aircraft under lock and key and retired to their bedroom to write out their reports.

Danny wondered whether they had learned anything from the examination so far and if they had found the lost strut or had any clues as to what had happened to it. But they were even more closemouthed than before. If they found any clues or reached any conclusions as to the cause of the accident, they were keeping that information to themselves.

Although Danny was curious about the cause of the plane crash, he knew he would find out nothing from the men who were working on the mystery.

The FAA inspectors came out of their room presently and challenged Danny to a game of Monopoly. They started before supper, but when the dishes were done, they quit and started over, so Danny's mom could join them. It was eleven o'clock when they called a halt to the game for the night.

Danny was interested at the start, but as time went on, his thoughts drifted to Matt. His friend had been so excited about the visit of his mom and had been eager to talk to her about getting things patched up between herself and her husband. He had even asked

Danny to pray about it—that she would listen when he told her what was troubling him.

Yet, Matt hadn't mentioned it all day. And there had been plenty of opportunity. Danny couldn't help wondering what had taken place. Things must not have gone so well for him.

That night as he crawled into bed, he prayed for a long while for Matt, that he would be able to talk to his mom about stopping the divorce and reestablishing their family once more. But Danny was still as troubled when he finished praying as he had been at the start.

CHAPTER 7

DOESN'T GOD CARE?

Dr. Granville and his associate spent several days at the wreckage, going over it piece by piece. At first, they talked with Carl about some of their findings, but as they neared the conclusion of their investigation they became strangely secretive.

They hadn't been able to pinpoint the cause of the accident, they told him. In fact, insofar as they knew, the plane hadn't yet been positively identified. The numbers were false, and no flight plan had been filed. The authorities were still trying to learn the identities of the two men who had been killed in the crash.

Wednesday afternoon they concluded their work at the site of the smashup and wanted to get Matt to radio for a plane to pick them up the next morning. Dr. Granville was going to make the trip to the Fuller place himself, but Danny volunteered to go for him.

"Matt's been home sick all week," he said. "I'd like to see how he's doing."

"I won't argue with you about that, Danny," the chief inspector said. "We've been out in the cold all day. It'll feel good to stay in here by the fire."

Danny put the message in his shirt pocket and crossed the ice to Matt's grandmother's on his snowmobile.

He was surprised to see that his friend was up and dressed, sitting near the stove, listening to the radio. He looked up when Danny came in but only grunted.

"Feeling better?"

Matt shrugged indifferently. "I guess so."

"Mrs. Edgren was asking about you today."

His lips curled. "So?"

Danny didn't know what was wrong with his friend, and he couldn't ask with Mrs. Fuller sitting there. It might be something Matt didn't want her to know about. He set the book pack on the table and removed its contents.

"I brought home your books and assignments so that you won't get so far behind."

Matt Barton did not thank him. "Big deal!"

"Matthew!" his grandmother scolded. "Don't be like that! Danny's just trying to help."

He raised his gaze defiantly. "So, he's helped! Big deal!"

Danny ignored Matt's ill temper and took the message from his shirt pocket.

"Dr. Granville asked me to come over and have you send for a plane to pick them up in the morning."

Matt took the message and started for the room where he kept his ham radio. The door was shut, and he was seated at the radio before he spoke.

"Did they finish?" he asked.

"They're through here," Danny answered. "Now they've got to go to the lab and finish the job."

"Find out anything yet?"

"You know how Dr. Granville is. He never tells anybody anything."

Matt acted as though he was about to comment, but instead, he turned his attention to the radio. He got in contact with a ham in Baudette and sent the message.

"Have him call Mr. Rankin to see if he can come, then get back to us."

While they were waiting, Matt slumped in his chair as though the burden he was carrying was too great for him.

"Something eating on you?" Danny asked after a time.

Matt shook his head. He acted as though he was about to lapse into silence again, but he pulled himself erect, eyeing Danny. "A lot of good it did to pray!" he blurted.

"I've always found that it helps," Danny replied evenly.

"For you, maybe. But not for me! God doesn't *care* what happens to me, or even what I want!"

"That's not true," Danny countered. "It tells us somewhere in the Bible that God even cares about the sparrows. If He's concerned about a little bird like that, He cares about you and me."

Matt stood and went over to the frosted window. Even though it was covered over, he stared at it. Then he faced his friend.

"You talked me into praying that Mom and Dad would get things worked out between them," he began. "You even volunteered to pray about it yourself. And you got your folks to pray.

"I believed you!" he continued bitterly. "I was sure all that praying would do something. But it hasn't! They're farther apart now than they've ever been!"

Danny was slow in answering. "That doesn't mean God isn't working!"

"It does to me! You know what?" His voice raised angrily. "Mom's already filed for divorce! Now, she's waiting 'til it's final so she and that Osborne dude can get married! A lot of good all your praying has done!"

Danny was slow in answering. He knew God didn't always give us the answer to our prayers that we wanted, but he had never come up against anything quite like this before. He didn't know what to say.

"I'd like to have you talk to my dad," he said at last. "I'm sure he'd be able to help you."

"It's too late for *anyone* to help now! Don't you understand? She's going to *marry* that stupid character in two or three weeks! That's the last thing she told me before they took off for Denver. When that happens, it'll be too late! Dad and her'll *never* be able to get back together again."

Danny Orlis left the Fuller house shortly and made his way back home. As he was leaving, Matt told him he would be back in school the next day.

"Wait for me. OK?"

"Right on!"

"And thanks for bringing over my books."

"Sounds like you won't need them now."

"I'll do a little studying tonight." He flashed a quick smile and closed the door.

Danny felt better after that. At least his friend wasn't mad at him. He realized now that Matt probably hadn't been mad at all. He was upset about his mom and the fact that she was going to be married to someone other than his dad.

On the way home, Danny thought that he should have told Matt he would be praying for him, but he realized that wouldn't have had any effect. Not the way he felt about prayer.

That night Danny prayed longer and harder for Matt than ever before. Only this time he prayed differently. He asked God to bring Matt's folks back together, and he also asked Him to forgive Matt for feeling that God didn't care about him. And he prayed that Matt would soon confess his sin and put his trust in Christ.

When Matt got to Danny's, he was as discouraged as he had been the night before, though he tried not to show it.

Mrs. Edgren was glad to see him in school and told him she wanted him to stay for a few minutes when classes were out that afternoon.

"I want to go over your assignments and work out a schedule so you can get your work caught up."

He nodded wordlessly.

"Hey, you look wiped out," Don Clark said with a grin as they left the school building for recess.

"You would, too, if you had a stack of homework three feet high."

Don sidled closer to him and lowered his voice. "I've got something that'll take care of *all* your troubles."

"Even the homework?"

"Even the homework."

"The only thing that would be is someone to do it for me, and Grandma'd *never* allow that."

"That's not what I'm talking about." That superior little grin came back as he pulled two hand-rolled cigarettes from his pocket and held them out to Matt.

He stared down at them. "Where'd you get the pot?"

"It don't make any difference where I got it. Want a couple of joints?"

Matt shook his head.

Don seemed irritated that his offer had been refused. "What's the matter?" he demanded. "Scared?"

"Me?" Matt laughed scornfully. "What's to be scared of?"

"You tell me." He pushed the marijuana cigarettes at Matt once more. "I know Danny's so religious, he's weird. I wouldn't even give *him* a chance like this. But I figured you were different. I didn't think you were chicken."

"Me, chicken?" Matt echoed. "I've smoked more of that stuff than you ever saw!"

"Prove it! If you're so great; prove it!" He thrust the cigarettes Matt's way once more.

Matt pushed them away as Danny came up to him and Don.

"Hey," young Orlis said, "what's this all about?"

"Nothing," Don muttered, walking away, his hands in his pockets. "Nothing at all."

Danny watched him curiously. "What's going on, Matt?" he asked.

Matt hesitated. It was obvious that he didn't want to say, but when Danny asked again, he told him.

"Man!" Danny exclaimed. "I knew he wasn't a Christian, but I sure didn't know he was into that stuff."

"It's not as bad as all that," Matt countered.

Young Orlis stared at him. At first, he could not believe he had heard his friend correctly. "What do you mean by that?"

"It's not what adults say it is," he continued. "They try to make out that it's something terrible. That you'll get hooked on it if you keep using it. They try to tell you that it dulls your mind and all sorts of things. The truth is, it won't hurt a guy as much as cigarettes or whiskey."

"I know better than that," Danny countered. "Pot leads to other drugs. That's been proven. And it does affect the mind. Studies have proved that too. And now many scientists think pot is a bigger cause of health problems, such as lung cancer, than cigarettes ever thought of being."

He was about to continue when the bell rang, and the kids started reluctantly for the building.

"I sure hope you never use that stuff, Matt."

Matt frowned. "Me?" he echoed, lying to his friend. "I've never used pot and I never will. I just don't buy all the bad things they say about it."

Don came up just then, and Danny couldn't answer his friend, but he thought of little else the rest of the day.

On the way home, he tried to get back to the subject of Don Clark and the marijuana he had offered Matt, but it was useless. Every time Danny mentioned Clark or the substance he was trying to get Matt to smoke, his friend changed the subject or sat quietly on the snowmobile as though he hadn't heard.

On most occasions, he would stop off at the Orlis place for a while before walking home. This time, however, he insisted on leaving immediately.

"I've really got to go, Danny," he said. "I've got a pile of studying to do, and I've got to get with it."

Danny knew that was true, but it seemed strange for Matt to be concerned about his lessons. He never had been any other time since he had known him.

Danny went into the house thoughtfully, still concerned about his friend. Mrs. Orlis came to the kitchen door.

"Where's Matt?" she asked.

"He said he had to get right home."

"That's too bad. I made some doughnuts this afternoon. I was going to send some home with him."

Danny went quickly to the door and looked out, but his friend was too far away to call to him.

After supper that night, they finished their Bible reading and were about to pray when Danny said he had a special problem he would like to have them pray about.

"Can you tell us what it is?" his dad asked.

"I—I'd rather not."

They didn't press him to tell them what was troubling him but prayed silently about the matter. They finished just before the seven o'clock news on the radio.

Danny went over and switched the radio on just in time to hear the announcer launch into Dr. Granville's report about the accident of a light plane on the Lake of the Woods that claimed the lives of two men.

"Dr. Granville, chief inspector for the FAA in this area, refused to comment today on a report from usually reliable sources that the Cessna 180 that crashed a week ago on the Northwest Angle of the Lake of the Woods had been sabotaged.

"The registration numbers on the plane were false, but it was traced by the serial number on the engine to the Mattson Flying Service operating out of Bemidji, Minnesota. Thomas Mattson and his chief mechanic, Nils Olson, both gave sworn statements that the plane had been properly marked when it left their hangar. It was rented for two weeks to a man by the name of Peter Cook from Fargo, North Dakota, for a business trip to Duluth, International Falls, and Winnipeg, Ontario, Canada.

"Cook's body has been positively identified. The passenger was Ramon Gonzales, a Colombian citizen now living in Miami, Florida. Unconfirmed reports link the two men to a drug smuggling operation, with connections in South America, Europe, Canada, and the United States...."

When the news was finished, Carl Orlis switched off the radio. "So that's what it was all about," he said.

"They didn't mention the money found in the plane," Danny observed.

Carl nodded thoughtfully. "That's right. I wonder why."

CHAPTER 8

"CHICKEN"

The next few days, Danny saw that there was a change in Don Clark. Before then he had paid no attention whatsoever to Matt. Now he stayed close to him whenever he could. He sought him out on the grounds before school and at recess. Even at noon, he managed to be with Matt. He shouldered past Danny and led Matt to a corner of the room, some distance away from the other kids.

There was only one possible reason for all of that attention, Danny realized. He was trying again to get Matt to use pot. Prayerfully, Danny determined that wasn't going to happen. At least it wouldn't if he could help it.

"You've got to be careful around Don," Danny warned him.

Matt bristled loyally. "He's a good Joe."

"Maybe so, but you know what he's trying to do, don't you? He wants to get you on grass."

The younger boy frowned. "He talks a lot, but that's about all it is."

"The other day he had a couple of joints he tried to give you," Danny reminded him. "That sounds like more than *talk* to me."

"A couple of joints?" Matt echoed scornfully. "If it's like most of the pot you'd be apt to find in a place like this, I could smoke both of them without feeling anything. You take that Mexican stuff that comes into the city where I used to live before the folks broke up, that was something else! You can get a high just lighting up."

Danny's eyes narrowed. He had suspected Matt was lying when he protested that he had never used marijuana, yet defended its use strongly. Now he was positive that his friend hadn't told the truth. Only someone who had actually used marijuana would be so knowledgeable.

"Just be careful," Danny warned aloud.

"I can take care of myself," Matt blurted.

Danny continued to pray for his friend with renewed fervor.

Young Barton continued to protest that Don and he were just friends. And, on some occasions, that seemed to be true. They talked in normal tones about baseball or hockey or fishing through the ice. At other times, Don bent his head close to his new friend and lowered his voice to a thin whisper. Whenever that happened, Danny joined them.

"It's *you* again!" Don muttered in disgust. "Bug off!"

Danny smiled pleasantly.

"I said, 'bug off!'" Don retorted irritably. "We don't need you around here! Get lost!"

"It's a free country."

By this time, Don's anger was building. "How many times do I have to tell you? We don't *want* you here! Go on! Leave us alone!"

Danny did not move. To do so would leave Matt in Don's hands, under the pressure of going back to smoking pot.

Don Clark got to his feet and clenched his fists. "Want me to *make* you?" he blustered.

"Any time," Danny countered evenly. It wasn't that he wanted to pick a fight with Don. He didn't care to fight with anybody, but this was worth fighting for, if it came to that.

Young Clark stepped forward, hesitantly, eyeing Danny's powerful arms and lean, well-muscled body.

"Danny's OK," Matt spoke for the first time.

The other boy wasn't sure he agreed with that. "I don't like having him stick his big nose into *our* business."

Nevertheless, he sat down once more, mumbling to himself.

After that, Don seemed to lose interest in Matt. Young Barton surely noticed the cooling of the other boy's friendship, but he said nothing to Danny about it—at least for several days.

During that period, Don directed his attention toward three other boys his age. The twins, Richie and Mickey Horton, and Heath Irwin were soon with Don constantly. They walked to school together and spent the recess periods and lunch hour off in a corner, talking in guarded tones.

On one occasion, they came to school early, and when Danny and Matt arrived, they were sitting on the front steps, a silly grin on their faces.

"Here comes that 'chicken,'" Don said, indicating Matt with a slow, exaggerated wave of his hand. "And he's got his 'mama' with him." He turned to his companions. "Did you know that Danny watches over little Matthew to see that he doesn't get into trouble?"

"Lay off!" Matt warned.

Heath's grin broadened. "If you weren't such a chicken, Matt," he said, "we could show you a real good time. Couldn't we, Don?"

"But we wouldn't show Danny," Clark broke in. He spoke slowly, as though his lips had difficulty forming the words. "Danny's so religious, he's *weird*."

"You guys're *stoned*." Danny Orlis exclaimed.

Don drew himself erect. "We've had a few joints," he said. "What're you going to do about it? Run to Mrs. Edgren?"

"You do," Richie broke in, "and you'll be sorry!"

"Relax, Rich," Danny said. "I'm not going to squeal on you. I won't have to."

"What do you mean by that?" the other boy asked defensively.

"You'll squeal on yourselves."

They stared his direction momentarily, having difficulty understanding what he meant.

"Squeal on ourselves?" Heath repeated. "How stupid can you get?"

"Yeah," Mickey put in, "if you two weren't so chicken, you could be having a ball with us." He glanced at Don. "Isn't that right?"

"Not Danny," the self-styled leader of the quartette said. "He's *weird*."

"Let's get out of here," Matt said, taking his friend by the arm.

"Chicken," Heath called after him, cackling loudly. "Chicken!"

Once they were around the school building, Matt turned to Danny. "Thanks," he said.

"For what?"

Their eyes met.

"You know."

Danny realized, then, that Matt had been aware of the fact that he was determined to break up the growing friendship between himself and Don Clark.

"At first, I thought it had to be because you were jealous. Today I saw *why* you were so anxious to keep me from being his friend. I could have been one of those dudes sitting on the schoolhouse steps."

"And you'd have been headed for big trouble, just like they are."

Matt frowned. "You don't know the half of it."

Danny was curious as to what he meant, but Matt didn't volunteer an explanation, and he didn't ask for one. He figured his friend would tell him if he wanted him to know.

Silently, Danny Orlis thanked God that He had protected Matt from dope. But, even as he did so, he knew the battle wasn't over yet. It wouldn't be over until Matt had confessed his sin and trusted Christ as his Savior. Then he would have a sound foundation for a life free from dope and liquor and things like that.

By the time the teacher and the other kids got to school, Don and his friends had better control of themselves, though Heath was given to a silly giggle every time someone said something. Even a remark by one of the older girls that the radio weather forecast was for snow over the weekend touched off a spasm of giggling. He laughed as though it was the funniest joke he had ever heard. The other kids stared at him, unable to figure out what had happened to make him so silly.

Mrs. Edgren glared. For an instant, Danny thought that Don and his friends were about to be unmasked. However, she rapped on the oak desktop with her ruler, and Heath straightened his lips forcefully, managing to suppress his giggling.

Later, the teacher directed her attention to one of the other boys in the quartette. "What is the matter with you, Richard?" she asked. "I've never seen you act like this before."

Fear swallowed his strange behavior, and he sat up straight, folding his hands on the desk in front of him. Don stared at his friends, warning them to more conventional behavior. They got the message conveyed by his eyes, and, with difficulty, were able to maintain control of their actions. By recess, they were almost themselves, and after a few minutes out in the brisk, cold morning wind, their heads were comparatively clear.

That afternoon when recess was over, Matt passed the quartette, huddled together along the south side of the schoolhouse where they were out of the wind. He hadn't intended to listen in on their conversation, but he couldn't help overhearing them. They were too involved in what they were talking about to be aware that anyone was close, and their voices grew somewhat louder.

"You're sure there's *more* over there?" Heath asked.

"There was a lot of it in the cabin when I was there."

"You should've grabbed a package."

"I could have," Don continued, "but I thought I heard someone coming. We'll go over and get more tomorrow."

With that, Matt was out of hearing. He turned the words over in his mind, excitement gripping him. He could scarcely wait for school to end for the day so he could share the information with Danny. The last hour dragged endlessly. He thought it would never be over. At last, however, Mrs. Edgren dismissed school for the day.

The kids rushed to the back of the building, where they pulled on their boots and jerked their parkas off the hooks. It was the same hurry to get outside every day, but Friday seemed to be special—a day when getting home carried a new sense of urgency.

"What time do you want to get together, Don?" Richie asked from the schoolhouse steps, his cheeks flushed with excitement.

"How does nine-thirty grab you?"

The other three nodded in agreement.

"Fine," Don said. "We'll get together at the usual place."

As he spoke, he saw that Matt Barton was eyeing him questioningly.

"Chicken," he murmured under his breath.

Matt felt the color creep up into his cheeks, and his fists clenched. *One of these days,* he said inwardly, *I'm going to lose control of myself and plow into Don, even if he is bigger.* He didn't know how much more of that he could take.

"Don't pay any attention to him," Danny said.

A contemptuous grin split Don Clark's features. "That's right. Go home with Mama's little helper! Chicken!"

Deliberately, Danny turned his back and strode over to the snowmobile. He turned the key and the starter engaged, turning the engine over slowly, dragged down by the cold.

"Think it's going to start?" Matt asked.

For answer, Danny tried again. It coughed nervously, backfired, and took off with a roar.

They sped over the snow and ice in the direction of home.

They had gone a mile or more when Matt leaned forward and told Danny to stop. He reduced the speed quickly.

"What's wrong?"

"I've got to tell you something."

Danny Orlis closed the throttle to idling speed and shifted into neutral. The snowmobile crept to a halt.

"Now," he said, "what is it?"

Excitedly Matt related what he had overheard.

"So," he concluded, "I figure Don found some pot somewhere, and tomorrow they're going back for more."

Danny pursed his lips. "Do you suppose that has something to do with the wrecked plane?" he asked.

"It could, for a fact. Maybe those two guys were coming in to buy a plane load of grass. That would account for that briefcase filled with money. Only they had that accident before they could make their buy. So, the stuff is still stashed away somewhere."

"But where?" Danny asked.

"Don knows. He found it."

Danny kicked the snow with his boot. "It's *got* to be somewhere in the general area of the Clark home," he said.

"That's the way I figure. And tomorrow they're going over to the place where he found it."

Danny saw what his friend was driving at. "And you want us to follow them. Is that it?"

Matt's grin was wide.

"Right on!"

CHAPTER 9

THE MISSING STRUT

The following morning, Matt got up while it was still pitch dark outside. He fixed his own breakfast and hurried across the ice to the Orlis home. His grandma hadn't been certain she ought to allow him to traipse off to Danny's so early in the morning, but he was able to convince her that Carl and Mary Orlis were *always* up early, and they wanted him to come.

He didn't tell her that Danny was the only member of the Orlis family who knew he was coming that particular Saturday morning, but he didn't think it made that much difference. Every time he left, Mary Orlis told him that he was welcome any time. And he knew that was true. Everybody liked to go to the Orlis house.

It had turned colder during the night, and the wind snarled over the rough ice and numbed his cheeks. He pulled his scarf tighter about his nose and quickened his pace.

No one was about, especially in that thinly populated section of the Lake of the Woods. Nevertheless, Matt glanced around uneasily. Somebody had to have brought that cache of marijuana into the Angle. It didn't get there by itself. And, if they brought it in, there was a chance that they were still in the area. Guys like that did most of their work at night when they wouldn't be seen.

What if he ran into those dudes on the way to Danny's?

He shivered and wished he was already there or that he hadn't come so early. He was glad when he got close enough to Pine Creek to see the lights in the Orlis windows.

Matt sat up to the table and ate a second breakfast with the Orlis family. When they were finished, he helped Danny with the chores he had to do every morning; then they were on their way.

"I was afraid your grandma wasn't going to let you come," Danny said as they pushed the snowmobile out of the shed and filled it with mixed gas and oil.

"No sweat."

The false dawn was beginning to light the far horizon, giving promise that the sun was on its way. Gray streaks on the eastern skyline began to banish the worst of the darkness, and the boys were able to make out the faint silhouette of trees on shore and the shape of a small island to their right, as they traveled.

By the time they drew near the Clark cabin, the sun was shining through the thin, silvery sheen of clouds. There was no warmth in its rays, but daylight was upon them.

"What're we stopping here for?" Matt asked.

"We've got to stash this snowmobile away. We'd never be able to get close to those dudes with as much noise as it makes."

Matt nodded. He had never thought of that.

They moved slowly along the thickly wooded shore, looking for a suitable place to hide the machine. After several minutes, they came upon a stretch of ice that would leave no trail to shout the change of direction the snowmobile took, heading off into the thick bush.

The instant they left the lake, however, the machine cut a track in the snow. The boys hid the Bearcat some distance from the lake and covered it with branches. Then they brushed out the tracks with pine boughs.

"That isn't too good a job," Matt said uneasily. "Anybody who comes along would see it."

"They'd have to be looking close," Danny answered. "Most guys would go right by without even noticing."

His friend wasn't too sure of that, but he didn't see any other solution if they wanted to follow Don and his friends to see where the marijuana was hidden. Danny and Matt didn't know where Don and the twins and Heath were to meet, but they went toward the Clark home until they saw a set of footprints that came from the clearing and led off through the woods.

"Now, all we've got to do is to follow him," Matt said, triumphantly.

Danny held a finger to his lips in warning. "S–S–Sh! Sound carries a long way in the wintertime. We've got to be careful, or we'll give ourselves away!"

They walked in silence along the path, following Don's footprints in the snow. A few minutes later, as they approached a small clearing, they could hear voices. Danny stopped momentarily, listening.

"It's them," he whispered. "I can hear Heath."

They left the trail and moved cautiously through the bush until they were close enough to understand what the other boys were saying.

"All set?" Richie asked.

"Right on. Only keep an eye out. The guys who stashed that stuff are apt to be around these parts, and they may be back any time."

"Man!" Heath exclaimed in that thin, high-pitched whine. "Maybe we'd better change our minds."

"No way!" Don broke in. "We're not giving up now! All we've got to do is set a couple of guys to watching while the other two go in and get two bundles of grass. I know right where it is. It won't take us two minutes!"

"OK, but I'm not too keen on having those dudes catch us in their cabin."

"Neither am I. But look at all that good pot we can get."

With that, Don led his companions into the bush in a southwesterly direction. As soon as they were out of sight, Danny turned to his companion.

"I know where they're heading," he said confidently.

Matt was surprised. "You do?"

"There's an old trapper's cabin over that way—the only one within several miles. That's *got* to be it."

Matt started forward impetuously. "What're we waiting for? Let's get moving."

"We'd better let them get ahead of us," Danny told him. "Those dudes are going to keep a close watch for anyone getting close to them—especially going in."

They waited for five minutes before following Don and his friends. Then they moved forward cautiously, taking care to avoid stepping on sticks or branches that would crack noisily under their weight and give them away. They had left the trail and were tramping through the bush, which made the going slower for them than the boys they were following. They were just approaching the clearing with the old cabin in the center when Don and Heath came out the open window.

"Where is it?" the twins cried, seeing that the other two had nothing in their hands.

"We were too late!" Don said. "Whoever left the stuff here came and got it!"

"All of it?"

"All but a few bits of broken leaves. Not even enough for a joint."

"You should've got it while you had the chance," Richie protested.

"I know that now, but there's nothing I can do about it."

They made their way slowly up the trail, leaving the window open and the screen loose, except for the tacks along one side.

"Hey," Heath exclaimed. "We didn't even close the window and put the screen back like it was."

"Why should we? There's nothing inside."

"If those dudes come back, they'll know right away that we were in there."

"No way. They cleaned things out. They're not coming back. But, even if they do, they won't know it was us. All they'll know is that *somebody* got in there and was snooping around. Let's get out of here! I've got a little pot left. The whole day won't be shot."

Danny and Matt crouched tensely in the bush and waited until they were certain Don and the others were gone and weren't coming back. Then they stood erect.

"That was a waste!" Matt exclaimed, stretching to get the kinks out of his knees. "The grass is *gone*!"

"At least we know it was in the cabin a few days ago.

"But the dudes who left it here are probably long gone," Matt added. "Not that it makes me feel bad." He shivered at the thought of being caught in the cabin and would have started back along the path, but Danny stopped him.

"Let's have a look inside. OK?"

The boys approached the log structure and for a moment stopped before the door.

"Why do you suppose Don looked inside in the first place?" Matt asked. "It's such an *old* building."

Danny pointed to the shiny new padlock and hasp. "He probably wouldn't have if it hadn't been for that. This cabin has stood empty for at least four or five years. The lock and hasp that used to be on it were so rusted anyone could tell they'd been put on a long time ago. The new stuff shouts that somebody put something inside they didn't want anyone else to know about."

Matt nodded. "That makes sense. I suppose he was going by this way, saw the new padlock, and got so curious he broke in."

But Danny was scarcely listening. He pulled the old, rusted screen to one side, pushed the hinged window out of the way, and crawled in. His companion did the same.

"There's sure nothing in here," Matt said, looking around.

But Danny continued to search the cabin. He went over to the bed, lifted one corner of the lumpy cotton mattress, and looked through the link springs at the rough floor beneath. But there was no sign of anything there.

"We heard Don," Matt continued. "There's nothing in here. We'd just as well get on our way."

Danny agreed that there was no good reason for remaining inside and trying to search an obviously empty cabin, but there were things that bothered him—things that left questions in his mind.

"There's *got* to be a better hiding place than anything we've seen," he observed. "Marijuana is worth a lot of money, and it sounded to me as though they had quite a pile of it. They wouldn't leave anything like that out in the open so anybody who looked in the window could see it. They'd have that stuff out of sight."

"It might be in that airtight heater."

Danny lifted the tin lid, but the stove was empty, except for a few sticks of kindling. "No way."

They continued the search.

"You know," Matt said at last. "This is stupid. If those guys come back and catch us in here, we'll be blamed for stealing their pot and everything."

"We'll go in a sec."

Danny was about to leave when he noticed that the kitchen table was sitting on a faded old piece of linoleum. He pulled the table to one side and moved the piece of floor covering to reveal a trapdoor in the rough pine floor.

"Here we are!" he cried triumphantly.

Beneath the door was an opening that led to a root cellar about four feet deep and extending almost the width of the cabin. He didn't have a flashlight or matches, but he lowered himself into the small cellar, blinking as his eyes struggled to adjust to the dim light.

Like Don said, the marijuana was gone, except for a few leaf fragments and a smattering of dust. There were a number of pelt boards standing along an earthen wall, a dozen rusted traps, and the shriveled remnants of a ham that the trapper had forgotten when he left that spring, several years before.

Danny stooped and picked up a dried marijuana leaf, crumbling it between his fingers. He stared at it momentarily, thinking about all the problems and heartaches pot caused. As he looked up, he saw a long object wrapped in an old blanket on the floor. He uncovered one corner and shouted to Matt.

"I've found the missing strut!"

Matt jumped into the hole beside him and peered over his shoulder.

"Are you sure?"

"Look for yourself!"

For a moment or more, their eyes were fixed on the missing aircraft part. The end that held the ski in place was gone. And they knew why! The strut had been sawed more than half in two an inch above the ski! Bouncing on takeoff had broken it most of the way—so far that the metal broke completely during the flight.

"That was deliberate!" Matt cried.

"You can say that again!"

"What're we going to do?" he continued. "Take it with us?"

Danny shook his head. And in that moment, fear gripped him. The men who had been using that cabin were desperate. If they came back and caught him and Matt, it would be too bad.

"We'd better get back home and tell Dad. He'll know what to do!"

CHAPTER 10

"YOU'LL SQUEAL ON YOURSELVES"

Danny and Matt crawled out the window hurriedly, but they took time to pull it shut and re-nail the screen over the opening. They were in such a hurry that they did a crude job that would not have deceived anyone who examined it closely, but they counted on the fact that anyone coming to the cabin would have other things on his mind. Anyone, that was, except Don or his companions. They would know, in an instant, that someone had been there. But they would think it was the guys who hid the marijuana in the first place. And they would get out of there fast.

"What do we do now?" Matt asked, as they rushed along the path toward the place where their snowmobile was secreted.

"Get back to the house and tell Dad about the strut," Danny answered. "I know he'll get in touch with Dr. Granville right away."

"What about Don and those dudes with him?" Matt asked. "Do we tell on them, too?"

Danny thought about that. What they had done was wrong. There was no question about that. They probably deserved to be squealed on, but he didn't want to be the one to do it unless he had to.

"We're not going to lie to protect them," he said, "but I don't want to get them in a jam if we don't have to. Everybody in school'd be down on us."

Matt nodded in agreement. He felt the same, except that lying didn't bother him all that much. Not if they had a chance to get away with it. He guessed that was one of the ways he differed from Danny.

They backed the Bearcat out of its hiding place and raced home. Carl Orlis saw them coming and sensed something was wrong. Danny was speeding, for one thing, lurching over the snow and ice much faster than usual. For another, he was leaning forward tensely. Even Matt, who was on behind, seemed to be trying for more speed. Carl went to the bank of the frozen creek and waited.

Hurriedly, Danny blurted out what they had found.

"What did you do with that strut?" he asked when his son finished the account.

"It's right where we found it."

"You did the right thing. I'm sure Granville wouldn't have wanted you to take it away from there." He was so excited about their finding the strut that he asked no questions about why they had gone to the old cabin in the first place. They might come later.

"We figured you'd want to radio Dr. Granville," Danny said.

"That's exactly what we're going to do." He turned toward the house. "I'll tell mom where we're going."

On the way to Mrs. Fuller's, Carl Orlis worked out a message to Dr. Granville that would inform him of the fact that he was urgently needed at the Angle, without revealing anything to those who were involved in the plot to cause the plane to crash, in case they chanced to be monitoring Matt's radio frequency.

"Come back for ice fishing," he radioed. "Urge you to return as quickly as you can."

They waited in the bedroom where Matt's radio was set up until the ham on the other end had phoned Granville and relayed his answer.

"Sorry I can't make it. Two friends want to come. Will arrive Monday morning. Signed, Doc."

They were surprised that Granville wasn't coming back himself, but like Danny's dad said, that wasn't their problem. They had notified him. What he did about it was up to him.

Monday morning, when Matt and Danny got to school, Don Clark was waiting for them, his youthful features twisted with anger. He sidled up to Matt and whispered guardedly, "We'll see you guys at recess."

Matt caught the hostility in his voice. "What's the matter with right now?"

"Heath and the twins aren't here yet."

"What's the matter?" Matt asked. "Do you have to have somebody else fight your battles?"

Don's temper exploded. "I don't have to have *nobody!*" he snarled, grabbing Matt Barton by the parka hood and jerking him close.

Matt wrenched away and gave Don a shove, sending him sprawling backward in the snow. Clark leaped to his feet and came plowing in, his fists flailing. Matt stepped nimbly to one side and caught him with a sharp right to the cheek that snapped his head to one side and raised a livid welt under his eye. It was difficult for them to fight, dressed as heavily as they were in parkas and snowmobile gloves, but that didn't stop them.

Don was so angry he was crying as he bore in, swinging his right. It missed Matt by four inches. That was the last blow of the brief battle. Mrs. Edgren flew out of the schoolhouse door and grabbed both of them.

"That's enough of that!" she snapped. "Both of you inside—immediately!"

"He started it!" Don stormed defensively.

"You know better than that!"

The teacher turned to the other boys who had been watching. "Who started the fight?" she demanded.

Nobody would answer her.

She turned to the girls. "It seems as though the boys didn't see a thing," she said, her tone icy. "Who started the fight?"

There was a brief hesitation.

"He did," Amy Myers said at last, pointing at Don.

"You're lying!" he snarled. "I did not!"

"You did so!"

With that, the other three girls who had been on the school grounds when the fight started, nodded their agreement with Amy. "Don Clark started it."

Mrs. Edgren relaxed her grip on Matt.

"Donald," she said, sternly, "go into the schoolhouse and wait for me."

"But I–"

"Do as I say!" She directed her attention to Matt after the bigger boy was gone. "And you, Matthew! Don't think you're out of this scot-free. I'll deal with you later!"

Once Mrs. Edgren was gone, and the other kids had drifted off in groups of two or three, talking about the fight, Danny went over to his friend.

"What was that all about?" Matt wanted to know.

Danny shrugged. "There's only one thing I can think of," he said. "And I don't see how that could be."

"Are you thinking they may have found out we followed them on Saturday?"

"Why else would he be so uptight? And he isn't just mad at you. Right at first, he mentioned me, too."

Danny and Matt were still talking when Don Clark came out of the schoolhouse, zipping up his parka. He glared at them but pushed past without saying anything. He started across the school yard toward the path that led to his home. He hadn't gone more than a few steps when Heath and the twins saw him.

"Hey, Don!" Richie called. "Wait up!"

"Can't!" he snapped. "I've got to split!"

They hurried over to him. "Something wrong?"

He nodded. "I've got to get the old man! That witch, Edgren, says I can't come back to school 'til I bring him to talk to her!"

Heath's eyes widened fearfully. "Did she find out?"

"Shut your trap!" He lowered his voice, and so did his companions. Danny and Matt could no longer hear them.

After a minute or more, he disappeared up the path, and his friends approached the schoolhouse.

"You guys!" Heath said, motioning to Danny and Matt with a jerk of his head. "Come over here.

We want to talk to you!"

They did not move. "We're not running away," Danny said evenly. "If you want to talk to us, come on over."

They swaggered up, hostility in every move. "We *know* what you did Saturday morning," Richie broke in belligerently.

"What did we do?"

"You must've thought we were stupid or something! We saw you dudes go back into that cabin after we came out."

Danny smiled. "So?"

His features darkened. "Don's old man's been on his back. Especially the last day or so. And we know why, don't we?"

"Suppose *you* tell us."

"You've been doing a lot of loose talking, and we don't like it! We're going to warn you just one time! You talk about us again and you'll be sorry."

"Right on!" Mickey blurted. "You squeal on us or Don, and you'll be in *real* trouble! Don't you forget it!"

Danny grinned and stood his ground. "Cool it, Mick," he said. "We haven't squealed on you, and we don't intend to."

"That's better!" he swaggered.

"But not because we're scared of you. We know what you're doing, but we don't have any real evidence—yet."

Mickey Horton's eyes narrowed uneasily. "What do you mean, 'yet?'"

"Just what I'm saying. If we get solid proof that you're using drugs and trying to get other kids into them, you can bet we'll tell somebody. And fast!"

Young Horton clenched his fist and inched forward. "You do and it'll be the *last* time you'll ever squeal on anybody."

"Like I said," Danny replied, his voice even, "we're not afraid of you, so you'd just as well forget that kind of talk. But I don't think we—or anybody else—is going to have to squeal on you."

"What's that supposed to mean?"

"You'll squeal on yourselves."

Matt was called into the building by Mrs. Edgren just then and informed that he would not be allowed to go out for recess for a week.

"Instead," she told him, "you must write this sentence 1,000 times, 'I will never fight with Don Clark or anyone else while I'm in school.'"

He groaned aloud.

"You're fortunate, Matthew," she said. "I could make you write that sentence 2,000 times."

He breathed deeply but said no more.

Danny expected Don Clark to be back at school with his dad before noon that morning, but he didn't show up all day. Danny and Matt talked about it on the way home.

"What do you suppose happened?" Matt asked.

Danny shrugged. "Maybe his dad wants to make him sweat a little before he lets him go back to school."

Matt was certain it was something more than that, but he didn't know what it could be.

As they neared Danny's home, they saw a plane taxi out of the creek mouth and wait for a time with the motor idling, to warm up. Then it took off smoothly, headed in the direction of the wrecked plane, and circled it at low altitude before winging south, climbing as it went.

"You just missed our friends from the FAA," Carl said.

"What'd they do?" Danny asked. "Go get the strut?"

His dad's face clouded. "I'm sorry, Danny," he answered, "but I can't tell you what they did. That is a secret I have to keep."

"But we're the ones who found it!"

"I know. And you'll get the whole story as soon as it can be told."

"That's not fair!" Matt said.

"Another thing. They don't want you boys going over to that old cabin anymore. Apparently, the men who are using it are very dangerous. They are afraid that something might happen to you—and so are mom and I."

The time came for Matt to go, and Danny followed him outside. "See you in the morning," he said.

Matt was reluctant to leave. "I—I wish you could take me."

Danny hesitated. "I'd like to, but Dad has some work he wants me to do. And after I get finished, I've got a pile of homework."

"I was just thinking. Don and those guys know we were in that cabin. Maybe those dudes who hid the dope there know too." He swallowed hard. "They might be just waiting for me to leave here and start home so–so they can grab me."

Danny breathed deeply.

"Hang in there, Matt," he said. "I'll talk to Dad." A moment later he was back. "Come on. I'll take you."

They covered the distance between the Orlis home and his grandmother's without incident.

"I'll come by for you in the morning too," Danny told him, "until this trouble's over."

"Awesome!"

The next morning when Danny drove up to the Fuller place on the Bearcat, Matt wasn't ready to go to school.

Mrs. Fuller came to the porch and invited Danny in. "Matt hasn't finished breakfast," she said.

He glanced at his watch. "It's getting late. We'll have to hurry, or we won't make the tardy bell."

"I'm sorry, but he had a hard night. When he got home, he had a letter from his mom. Her divorce is going to be final in three weeks, and she and Bob Osborne are going to be married the next day."

Silently, Danny prayed for his friend. He knew how hard it was for him. His mom had already told him she was going to be married as soon as she could, but he could hope that something would happen to stop it, as long as they weren't actually married. Now it was too late for his parents to get back together again.

"Dear God," Danny prayed, "help Matt to understand that You will give him the strength to accept this marriage, if he will only confess his sin and put his trust in You."

He was still praying when his friend came out.

"I suppose Grandma told you," he said bitterly.

"She did."

"Like I said, it did a *lot* of good to pray!"

Danny knew Matt shouldn't blame God for it, but he didn't know how to explain that to Matt so he would understand.

CHAPTER 11

"A LITTLE JOKE"

The boys trudged out to Danny's Bearcat, the snow squeaking noisily underfoot. Crisp arctic air stung their faces and whipped thin tendrils of new snow over the drifts. It was colder than before and gave hint that the mercury was going to shrink farther in the tube. But by this time, they were used to the cold weather and ignored it.

"See any strangers?" Matt asked uneasily, settling in place on the back of the snowmobile and pulling a wool scarf over his nose to meet the dark-lensed goggles he was wearing.

"Nope," Danny told him. "I didn't see anybody."

He twisted the key, and the starter growled as it turned the motor over. After several seconds, he stopped momentarily, and all was quiet once more.

"I got to thinking about those dudes," Matt continued. "They could grab us most anywhere."

"There's no need to worry about that," Danny said. "We don't even know if they're within a thousand miles."

"Maybe not," Matt answered doubtfully, "but I'll feel a lot better when they've been arrested and are in jail."

Danny didn't say it—he didn't want to get his friend any more upset than he was already—but he had to agree. He would feel a lot better when those dope smugglers had been arrested and taken away.

He started the engine, and they headed for school. When the boys got to the building, Don Clark and his dad were inside with Mrs. Edgren. The kids were milling curiously about. Time came for classes to start, and still they were not called inside. The Horton twins and Heath were particularly concerned.

They were talking softly, but Danny and Matt could hear every word.

"Slip over and peek through the window," Richie told his brother, "and see what's going on."

"It's *your* idea. *You* do it."

"You're taller than me," he retorted scornfully.

"Heath's taller than either of us."

"Don't look at me," their friend said. "You aren't getting *me* anywhere near those windows. That old lady Edgren's a witch! I don't want any more trouble with her if I can help it."

A tense silence gripped the trio.

"Don's old man is sure staying in there a long time."

"You can say that again," Mickey said. "Maybe he found out."

"He did," Heath added. "Caught Don smoking pot out in the barn Saturday after we got home. I guess he was stoned out of his tree. His folks were scared he was dying and were going to send for an air ambulance to fly him to the hospital when they realized what was wrong with him."

"Wow!" Richie exclaimed. "Do you suppose he squealed?" His voice quavered. "Dad would beat you and me half to death if he found out."

"You can say that again!" Mickey put in.

"Don said he didn't tell them anything, but he was scared when I talked to him yesterday morning before the fight. He was plenty scared."

The front door opened just then and Mr. Clark strode out, his features somber. He stormed down the steps and across the packed snow to the trail that led to his home. Don was nowhere to be seen, but Mrs. Edgren stepped out on the little porch, the bell in her hand. Her face was white and drawn, and she hesitated momentarily before ringing for the kids to come in.

Don was in his seat when Danny and Matt filed in with the others and took their places at their desks. The Clark boy had obviously been crying. His cheeks were stained with tears, and his lips trembled.

"I'll get even with you!" he whispered in Matt's ear. "You can't squeal on me to my old man and get away with it!"

Matt turned back to him. "Cool it, Clark!" he whispered. "We didn't tell on you, but it wasn't because we're scared of you or your friends."

Mrs. Edgren saw that he was talking and rapped sharply on her desk. "Matthew!" she ordered. "Turn around and be quiet! I'll not have talking in class."

Cheeks flushing, he did as she said, folding his hands on the desk in front of him.

At recess, both Matt and Don had to stay in. Mrs. Edgren separated them, putting them on either side of her in the front row. Usually, she went out with the kids. That day, however, she remained inside. Don glared at her darkly and started to write. "I will never fight with Matthew Barton or anyone else while I am in school."

Matt was hard at work, also, scribbling virtually the same sentence, except that the name was different. A thousand times was a lot of writing. The way he felt right then it would take him a month.

Shortly before recess was over, two tall strangers came to the school, went inside, and talked to Mrs. Edgren in low tones. They showed her their credentials and asked to talk to Danny Orlis and Matthew Barton.

"Matthew," she said, "would you please get Danny. These gentlemen would like to talk to you both."

Fear leaped to Don Clark's eyes as Matt scurried out the door and called to his friend. The other kids came to the door and peered in as the two men took Danny and Matt into the little library off the classroom. The door closed behind them.

Mrs. Edgren rang the bell to call the classes in from recess. They poured through the door, hurriedly, questions in their young faces.

"Who're those dudes talking to Danny and Matt, Mrs. Edgren?" Heath asked nervously.

"Those *gentlemen* are with the Narcotics Department of the government," she said. "They want to ask Danny and Matt some questions."

"What about?" Richie Horton put in.

"You'll have to talk to them about that."

Mickey squirmed nervously. "Why talk to them?" he demanded. "They haven't done anything like—"

"Like *what?*" the teacher persisted.

"Like—like—" he swallowed at the lump in his throat. "Like smoking pot." He hadn't intended to say that, but he was so upset he wasn't thinking straight, and the words popped out.

"Shut up!" Richie muttered under his breath.

Mrs. Edgren went over to them. "I think you had better tell me what this is all about. You say Danny and Matt haven't been smoking marijuana. Who has?" She glanced at Don, and his friends realized that she knew about him, at least.

"Nobody," Mickey lied quickly. "Nobody I know of."

"I'm going to have Mr. Marshal and Mr. Thompson talk to you when they have finished with Danny and Matt."

Both Heath and Richie Horton glared at Mickey.

In the library, Mr. Thompson took a small tape recorder from his pocket and placed it on the table they were sitting around. "Now," he said, "suppose you start at the beginning and tell us what happened last Saturday."

"We went over to the cabin," Danny said, "and saw that a window was open and the screen was off, so we went in. We found a trapdoor under a piece of old linoleum and opened it. There were some bits of marijuana leaves and the broken strut."

"You left the strut there, didn't you?"

He nodded.

"That's what I understood from the FAA inspector."

He asked a few more questions and thanked the boys for their help. The men had learned most of the story from Carl Orlis and the FAA.

"We'll get back to you later if we have any more questions," he concluded.

It was their plan to leave immediately, but Mrs. Edgren called them aside and told them about Mickey's remark. They called the four boys into the library and kept them there until noon. When the youthful quartette came out, they were grim-faced and shaken. Richie was blasting his twin brother as they went by Danny and Matt.

"You had to shoot off that big mouth of yours!" he snarled. "Now we *are* in a mess! Dad'll skin us alive!"

"They'd have found out anyway," Mickey retorted defensively. "You could see that! Those dudes mean business!" By this time, they were out of hearing range of Danny and his friend.

"What's that all about?" Matt asked curiously.

"Sounds like Mickey got scared and talked too much," Danny said.

His companion was silent momentarily. "It happened just like you said. They squealed on themselves."

"That's the way it happens lots of times."

When Danny returned home after taking Matt from school to his grandmother's late that afternoon, Mr. Marshall and Mr. Thompson were already there. They were going to be staying for the duration of their investigation. He asked if they had found the cabin, and Thompson nodded.

"It was exactly like you told us." Then he changed the subject.

The following afternoon, as the bell rang, Mrs. Edgren called Danny to her desk.

"I want to talk to you about the paper you were supposed to hand in for English today," she said.

His cheeks flushed. "Oh–oh. I forgot all about it."

"That is obvious." Her expression was cold and emotionless.

Matt got to his feet. He was glad somebody besides him was catching it from Mrs. Edgren. It seemed that he was in trouble with her almost every time he turned around.

"I'll wait for you outside," he said under his breath.

"Good enough."

One of the girls came in to see the teacher, and she took care of that before directing her attention to Danny. It was ten minutes or more before she was even able to talk to him. Matt was getting cold. He stamped his feet in the snow to get the circulation going and looked toward the schoolhouse. Another five minutes, he told himself, and he was going back inside, even if Mrs. Edgren didn't like having them in the building when classes had been dismissed for the day. When they were out of school, they were supposed to go home—immediately.

He was about ready to go in and brave her indignation when he heard a snowmobile roaring up the lake. The sound floated in on the wind; a full-bodied whine that shattered the silence as the machine blasted into view. He had never seen a snowmobile go so fast. While he watched, it lurched toward the school in a wide, sweeping curve, and came to a halt near Matt. There were two bearded men on the powerful machine. They were wearing snowmobile outfits, complete with crash helmets. Matt couldn't see their features well enough to tell what they looked like or how old they were.

"I think you're the guy we want to see," the driver of the powerful machine rasped.

"Me?" He glanced about desperately, but there was no one else in sight. "Why me?"

"You're the dude with the ham radio, aren't you?"

He started to lie to them, but there was something about their piercing eyes that forced him to tell the truth. He nodded weakly.

"Good. We were afraid we would miss you."

"I—I've got to go inside," he stammered. "I'll see you around."

"Just a minute! We only want to talk to you. You'll send a message for us, won't you?"

He frowned. "I—" His voice trailed off, swallowed by the wind.

For one of the few times in his life, Matt tried to pray. It didn't go very well, but it made him feel a little better.

"We came up here ice fishing, and we've got this friend back home who was supposed to come but couldn't make it."

"Yeah," his companion broke in. "And we thought we'd like to send him a message. We want to play a little joke on him."

"I can't do it now," Matt said lamely. "I'm waiting for my friend."

The driver flashed a quick smile.

"And he's in trouble with the teacher, eh?"

"I guess you could say that."

"That's OK. We'll see you in a day or two."

As Danny came out of the schoolhouse, they waved to Matt and whirled away. Matt stared after them, his uneasiness growing. They acted as though they were all right, but he couldn't quite believe they would go to all that trouble to play a trick on a friend.

CHAPTER 12

A DRESS FOR THE WEDDING

"**W**ho were those dudes?" Danny asked curiously as he approached his friend.

"Search me." Matt gestured expressively. "I've never seen either one of them before."

"For a minute I thought maybe they were the guys who'd hidden that grass in Pete Olsen's old cabin."

"You and me both," he said. "But they sure didn't act like they were trying to hide. They came up to me right out in the open, big as you please. Said they wanted me to radio back to the Twin Cities for them. They want to play a joke on a friend."

The boys got on the snowmobile.

"You going to do it?" Danny asked.

Matt laughed. "How can I? They went racing away without even finding out where I live."

Danny was quiet as they traveled back to Pine Creek. Maybe those guys forgot to ask Matt where he lived, he reasoned, and maybe they didn't *have* to ask. It could be that they already knew!

When they got to the Orlis home twenty minutes or so later, they were surprised to see Amanda Fuller in the living room waiting for them.

"Grandma!" Matt exclaimed. "What're you doing here?"

"Carl stopped by the house this morning," she said, "and I asked him to bring me."

The boy squinted narrowly. "How come?"

"I—I—" she stopped and started again. "I'm going to have to be away for a few days and—and I wanted to see if Danny could come over and stay with you while I'm gone."

"You've never done that before," he reminded her.

"I know. But—" she swallowed hard. "I want to go down to Minneapolis to buy a new dress."

He stared hard at her, as though she had just betrayed him. "You're going to Mom's wedding!" he exploded.

"She invited me and I'm going," she answered. "I don't approve, but after all, she is my daughter."

Hurt flecked his eyes. "Don't you *care* about getting her and Dad together again?"

There was a brief silence. "I wish I could make you understand," she said weakly.

"What's to understand? She'll *never* go back to Dad now!" He turned on his heel and strode outside, slamming the door behind him. For a moment, the people in the Orlis living room looked at each other uncomfortably.

"Don't worry, Amanda," Mary Orlis said gently, ignoring the tears in her friend's eyes. "Everything will work out all right."

"I feel so sorry for him."

"I feel sorry for you too." She leaned forward slightly. "We will be praying for both of you."

That didn't seem to impress Mrs. Fuller. She sat very still, staring at her hands folded in her lap. "I've prayed until I'm hoarse, but it hasn't done a bit of good."

"God doesn't always answer our prayers as quickly as we wish or in exactly the way we wish."

Matt's grandmother fell silent for a time.

Matt came back into the room, anger gone, but there was evidence of tears on his cheeks.

The way she talked at first, Danny and Matt thought she was going to Minneapolis right away, but she said she planned to wait until the following week. "I just had to get things worked out so I knew what I was going to do," she said. "I couldn't leave the house without someone to stoke the furnace, and I didn't want to leave you there alone. I had to see if Danny could come and stay with you."

"I could manage," he said stiffly. "The Ericksons live right there beside us."

"I'd feel better if Danny was with you."

"Me too."

Matt said no more to his grandmother about her decision to go to his mom's wedding, but he was strangely quiet as they sat at the breakfast table the next morning. Once or twice, she tried to talk to him about it, but he wouldn't let her.

"There's nothing to talk about," he snapped. "You're going to the wedding. It's no skin off my nose."

"She would like to have you come too."

His features darkened. "That'll be the day!"

Matt and Danny went to school as usual that day. When they got there, the place was alive with excitement. According to the kids at school, the government agents had taken Heath and the twins to their parents and talked with Don Clark and his dad.

"And they're in big trouble," Amy Myers said. "I ought to know. I live right next to the Hortons."

"What kind of trouble?" Danny asked.

"The twins can't play with Don or Heath, for one thing. They can't even walk to school with them. And they're on probation. They can't take part in any sports. And if they get into any more trouble of any kind, or if they're caught smoking pot or using any other drugs, they won't be able to go to school."

Matt turned to Danny. "If it hadn't been for you, I might've been in with those dudes. Don almost got me."

Young Orlis grinned. "But he didn't. That's the main thing."

That afternoon when Danny took Matt back home, a sleek new Yamaha 440 was there, parked near a clump of brush behind the house. It looked as though the driver had casually pulled in and stopped, but the snowmobile was almost hidden from view. The boys wouldn't have seen it at all if they hadn't decided to go to the back door.

"Hey, you've got company," Danny said.

Matt's pulse quickened. "Yeah. It's those two dudes who stopped me at school and wanted me to send a message to their friend in St. Paul."

"Ever see them before?" Danny asked uneasily.

He shook his head. "They said they were vacationing in the area and wanted to play a joke on somebody."

"Vacationing?" Danny echoed, his voice skeptical. "This time of year?"

"That's what I thought. Guess they like snowmobiling and cross-country skiing."

Danny was thinking about the drugs that Don had found in the old Olson cabin.

"Are you sure those guys are legit?" he asked.

Matt moved closer to him. "I suppose so. But I do feel sort of strange around them. Want to hang around for a while?"

Danny didn't want to stay. He had chores and some homework to do, but he read the concern in his friend's eyes. "I guess I can for a little while."

"Until those two leave—OK?"

"OK."

"I'll get rid of them as quick as I can."

The two men were sitting in the living room having tea and homemade rolls when the boys came in. The strangers had their helmets off, and their snowmobile suits were unzipped. Their boots were at the door.

"This is Mr. John Turner and Mr. Cleve Wilson," Matt's grandmother said, introducing him and Danny to the visitors."

"We've never met Orlis," the blond John Turner said, "but we met your grandson. How are you, Matt?"

"OK, I guess." He shifted from one foot to the other. "I suppose you want to send that message you were talking about."

"Yeah." Turner fished a grimy scrap of paper from his pocket. "This's all we could find to write it on. We're vacationing, you know, and didn't bring any writing paper."

Matt read the note. "Edie sends her love. Wishes you were here. Signed: Cleve."

"Jess Turlock used to work up here on a boat that came out of Warroad. He was going with an Edie Pomeroy who waited tables at the resort on Flag Island," Wilson said. "Ever since we planned this trip, we've been kidding him about beating his time."

"Actually," Turner put in, "I suppose she's been married to somebody else for three or four years. She tossed Jess over for another dude, and he got so mad he quit and went south."

Matt wasn't all that interested in the guy who was to receive the message. All he wanted was to send it and get rid of his visitors.

"It'll only take a minute," he told them.

As he took the message and sat down at the radio, Turner spoke again. "Will you have to give your call letters when you send it?" he asked.

For an instant, surprise flecked the boy's eyes. Surprise and questions. "Always," he said. He thought everybody knew that. "Why?"

Turner acted as though he realized he had gone too far and tried to back off. "No reason," he said. "I was just wondering if Jess would know how to get in touch with us." He forced a short, thin, mirthless laugh. "It's not much fun pulling a joke on somebody if he can't answer back."

Both men stood close by, listening intently while he sent the message. When the operator in Burnsville, a southern suburb of Minneapolis, repeated the message and the phone number it was to go to, the men relaxed. Wilson pulled a ten-dollar bill from his pocket and tried to hand it to Matt.

"I can't take any pay," he said. "I'm glad to do it."

"It's worth ten bucks to us, isn't it, Turner?"

His companion nodded. "Besides, we might want to send another message in a few days. If we've paid you for this one, you may be more willing to send another one."

"I can't take your money," Matt Barton answered.

They zipped up their snowmobile suits, pulled on their heavy, insulated boots, and started out the door, their helmets in their hands.

"Oh, yes," Turner said, as though the thought just came. "We may be getting a message from Jess ourselves, now that he's hearing from us." He chuckled thoughtfully. "If we do, write it down. We'll stop by to check when we're over this way."

When they were gone, Matt turned to Danny. "Thanks. I guess they were all right, but after everything that's happened…." He shuddered.

Danny didn't say anything to his friend. There was no need to get him upset on a hunch that may or may not be true, but Danny had the feeling that there was something phony about the two men. They were a little too nice and congenial—a little too correct in what they said—as though they were consciously trying to allay any fears or suspicion the boys might have.

He was still concerned as he turned the snowmobile around and rode back to the house on Pine Creek. It could be a coincidence that they were vacationing in the area at the same time the narcotics agents were looking for dope smugglers. That sort of thing happened all the time. Yet, he wondered.

Saturday morning, a message came in for Wilson and Turner from their friend in Burnsville. "Delighted to hear about Edie. Will radio her Tuesday evening at 22:00 hours. Tell her I can hardly wait. Signed Jess."

Later in the day, they stopped and picked it up. Again, they wanted to give Matt ten dollars.

"I can't take it," he protested.

The following afternoon, Matt came to the Orlis house for Danny.

"Grandma had me radio for Mr. Rankin to pick her up today," he said, "so I thought I'd better come over and have you come to stay with me."

"Fine. I'll get my clothes and books tomorrow."

Matt followed Danny into his bedroom. "Turner and Wilson were back yesterday. I'm glad I'm through with those dudes."

"Are you sure?" Danny asked.

"They picked up a message that came in from their friend and didn't say anything about sending another one, so I figured I'm through with them."

The boys had been back at the Fuller home only half an hour when the Cessna 180 flew in, landed on the ice in front of the house, and took Matt's grandmother to Minneapolis.

"I'll be back Wednesday or Thursday," she said.

They stood in the yard and watched until the plane was out of sight.

"I don't know why she has to go to that wedding," Matt blurted as he and Danny headed for the house. "Mom wrote begging *me* to come too, but *I'm* not going. If she thinks so much of that Osborne character, let her have him! She doesn't need to think I'll be there and make everybody believe I'm happy about it!"

"You wouldn't be showing everyone you approved of her marriage if you went to the wedding," Danny said. "You'd just be showing that you *love* her."

Matt stamped the snow from his boots and stepped into the kitchen. "I thought you and your folks didn't believe in divorce. That's what you told me!"

"We don't," he answered, "but the Bible tells us to honor our fathers and our mothers."

"Mom sure doesn't honor Dad."

"That doesn't mean you can treat her the same as she treats your dad."

Matt pulled out a chair and sat down. "You know, Danny," he said seriously, "I made a bargain with God, but He didn't keep His end of it."

"Maybe He didn't make a bargain with you," Danny said quietly.

"Maybe not." His face grew hard. "But I told Him I'd become a Christian and live exactly the same as you if He would bring Mom and Dad back together. And nothing happened."

Danny Orlis breathed deeply. "The way I look at it, God doesn't want you to become a Christian on those terms."

"What do you mean?"

"He wants you to confess your sin and put your trust in Him for salvation because you love Him, not because you get something you want."

Matt got up and strode to the window. "I don't get it!"

CHAPTER 13

TRAPPED

Monday afternoon when school was out, Danny and Matt went back to the Fuller place by snowmobile, stopping at the Orlis home on the way. The mail had come in an hour before, and Carl Orlis was in the little post office where he had just finished sorting it. When he saw the boys, he picked up a letter he had laid to one side.

"Here you are, Matt," he said, smiling genially. "I had an idea you and Danny would stop by on the way from school. I've got a letter for you."

The boy's eyes brightened.

"Maybe it's from Dad!" Then he saw the familiar feminine handwriting on the envelope. His excitement faded and hurt marred his features. "It's another letter from Mom!" He studied the envelope thoughtfully for a moment before turning and stalking outside. Danny followed him, surprised at the disappointment he showed.

"Aren't you *glad* to hear from your mom?" he asked curiously.

Matt stopped on the snow-packed path and turned to Danny. "I would be," he said, "but I already know what's in it. She's always raving about what a terrible guy Dad is and how happy we are all going to be when she gets married to that Osborne dude."

Danny saw the hurt in Matt's eyes and knew he should say something, but what could he tell his friend that would make things easier for him? Matt turned abruptly and started for the house. The moment Danny could have used to talk to him was gone.

The boys went inside for the milk and freshly baked cookies they knew would be waiting for them. Danny tried hard to find something to talk about that would take Matt's mind off his troubles, but his misery seemed to grow. He was silent in the Orlis home, except when he was asked a direct question. And for the first time, he failed to thank Mrs. Orlis— not even for the sack of cookies and doughnuts she sent along with them.

A few minutes later, they reached the Fuller house and parked the snowmobile in a small shed out back. Danny led the way inside, stopping on the steps to kick the snow off his boots.

"I'm about starved," he said. "What's for supper?"

"There should be something in the kitchen," Matt told him. "You can get started."

"I thought it was your turn."

"You're the one who's so hungry. I've got something else to do first."

Danny's eyes narrowed. "What's that?" he asked. "Read your letter?"

Matt frowned. "Don't push me! I've got to go down to the basement and stoke the furnace."

It was one of those new-type wood furnaces that burned for twenty-four hours on one filling. They had filled it the night before.

"Wait until after supper and I'll help you," Danny said.

"I'll manage." He flashed a thin smile at his friend and went to the basement. At the top of the stairs, he switched on a light, and the diesel power plant started, furnishing electricity for the house and outbuildings.

When Matt came back upstairs a few minutes later, he sat down at the kitchen table and took the crumpled letter from his pocket. The scowl on his face deepened as he read.

"This letter's sure not like the others!" he blurted. "It's worse!"

Danny stared at him wordlessly.

"Here, read it for yourself!" Matt thrust the scented stationery into his friend's hand.

"See what she's cooked up now. As soon as she and Osborne get back from their honeymoon, she wants *me* to leave Grandma's and go out to Colorado to live with her and her *new* husband!"

Danny studied the sheet of paper Matt had given him. He didn't want to read it, but Matt seemed to want him to, so he did. It was just like his friend said. Only it was easy to see that she was almost as upset as her son and was pleading desperately for him to treat her the way he had before the divorce.

"I'm not goin' to do it!" Matt exploded. "I don't care what she says! I'll run away first!"

Danny couldn't even guess the turmoil his friend was experiencing. His was a Christian home where there was not even any open quarreling. He couldn't imagine what it would be like to have his parents so angry with each other that they would decide that divorce was the only solution. But he knew there had to be a better way than running off.

"They'd only come and find you," Danny reminded him.

"Then I'd run away again!" His eyes pleaded with Danny for understanding. "*You* don't know what it's like!"

"You're right about that," Danny said. "I don't know what you're going through. But I know Someone who does. Someone who can help you."

Matt snorted. "*Nobody* can help me out of this mess except Mom, and she thinks she's so much in love with this Osborne dude that she doesn't care about Dad or me or Grandma or anyone else!"

"You're wrong when you say no one else understands or can help you. God does. He knows all about your heartache, and He *wants* you to come to Him."

Matt's eyes blazed. "If He wants to help so bad, why doesn't He? What's He waiting for?"

"You."

"That doesn't make sense."

"But it does," Danny continued. "God doesn't force Himself on anyone. He wants you to come to Him."

Matt Barton thought about that.

"I came to Him once," he said. "Remember? We prayed and prayed that God would bring my folks back together, but it didn't do a bit of good. In fact, things are worse than ever."

"God doesn't always answer our prayers exactly the way we want Him to, but He knows what's best for us."

Matt's features twisted painfully. "Anybody would know what's best for me!" he muttered. "But that doesn't do any good. It's not going to happen!"

Danny went to the kitchen table and sat down. His friend pulled out a chair opposite him and did the same.

"I don't know why God hasn't brought your parents back together, but I do know what He wants of you. He wants you to confess your sin and put your trust in Him. He wants you to become a Christian."

Matt pulled in a deep breath. "Then?" he asked. "Does that mean He'll stop Mom from marrying this dude and send her back to Dad?"

"That might not be what He will do. Like I said, He doesn't always work the way we may want Him to. But He will help you more than you have ever thought He could. He will give you the strength you need to accept the fact that your mom is marrying again, or whatever it is that He has for you."

Danny saw tears come to his friend's eyes, but he didn't mention them.

"The Bible says that He will not leave us comfortless. That means He cares what happens to us and wants to help us."

Matt pushed back his chair and got to his feet.

"God wouldn't want to save me," he murmured. "Not after all the things I've done." He hesitated momentarily. "You don't know it, but I've smoked pot and been stoned out of my skull on LSD and uppers and downers. Another kid and me got caught breaking into a grocery store to get money for dope. The only way the Fuzz would let me off on probation was for me to come up here to Grandma's." His lips curled bitterly. "I guess they figured there wasn't much trouble I could get into up here."

Danny didn't speak for a moment, and Matt continued.

"I suppose you and your folks won't want to have anything to do with me, now that I've told you that."

"I don't know why not. If you used dope when you were with me and tried to get me to use it, that would be different, I suppose. But we're sure not going to turn against you because you've done things in the past that you shouldn't have."

Matt came back and sat down, smiling slightly. "That's a load off my chest. I figured if you heard about the things I'd done back home, you wouldn't want to be my friend anymore, and I wouldn't have *anybody* except Grandma."

"The Bible says it doesn't make any difference what we've done in the past," Danny said. "If we confess our sin and ask Jesus to forgive us, He will. He gives us a clean heart. It's as though those terrible things had never happened."

His companion, who had been staring blankly across the room, fixed his gaze on Danny. "Do you really mean that?"

"God really means it! And that's a lot more important."

Matt had more questions. When they were answered, he was ready. They bowed their heads, and he prayed a short, halting prayer, acknowledging that he was a sinner and wanted to receive Christ into his heart.

They had just finished praying when there was a muffled sound on the back steps.

"What was that?" Matt demanded.

Danny shook his head. "Sounds like there's somebody out there!"

He started toward the door. "That couldn't be. Nobody comes here at this time of night."

As if in answer to his statement, there was a loud knock. With his hand on the knob, he turned back to Danny, fear creeping into his eyes.

Danny's lips parted, but he did not speak. He saw the knob turn and the door creaked open. Two men were standing there, grinning broadly.

"Hello, Matt!" one of them said. "We're back to have you send another message."

"We didn't hear your snowmobile," Matt said numbly.

"We left it across the island," Turner said. "Thought we'd surprise you."

"As a matter of fact," Wilson put in, "we saw snow-mobile tracks headed this way and figured you might have company, so we thought we'd take a look first."

"I do have company."

He nodded, his eyes narrowing. "Yeah. Another kid!" His expression changed. "Ain't you even going to ask us in?"

"I'm sorry," Matt began. He was about to lie to the men, telling them that his radio wasn't in working order when he remembered that he was a Christian now. "We haven't had supper. You'll have to come back tomorrow."

Wilson glanced at his companion. "I don't think we've got time."

"I reckon not," Turner growled. "It ain't goin' to take long to get that message on the way."

They pushed into the house and closed the door behind them.

"Give it to me," Matt said. "I'll see if I can raise somebody to phone it to your friend. They may not be on, you know."

"Oh, he'll be on," Turner said confidently. "I'd bet on it."

The four of them went up to the second-floor bedroom where Matt had his radio. He sat down at the controls.

"Here's the message," Turner said. "EDIE HAS A DATE TOMORROW NIGHT. MAKE IT WEDNESDAY. Signed: JOHN TURNER."

Matt switched on the radio and glanced up at Danny; then he directed his attention to the man who was sending the message.

"You don't expect us to believe that, do you?" he asked boldly.

Briefly, fear leaped to the man's eyes. "Believe what?"

"This message! It's a phony! Isn't that right, Danny?"

Danny winced. He didn't know what had gotten into Matt. He must have been out of his mind to blurt that out to those two ugly visitors, but now that Matt had started it, he couldn't desert him. And, especially, he couldn't lie.

"That's right. My dad's lived up here for more than twenty years. He knows *everybody* who's been in this part of the Lake of the Woods to live or work, and he says there isn't any Edie Pomeroy. Nobody by that name has worked at any of the resorts!"

Rage contorted Turner's face. "We tried to be nice to you. We wanted to keep you out of it, but if that's the way you want it, OK. Send that message and be quick about it!"

At that, Wilson pulled an ugly automatic revolver from a holster under his coat. "And if you know what's good for you, you won't try any funny stuff! Understand?"

CHAPTER 14

FREE AT LAST

"What if I *don't* send that message for you?" Matt demanded defiantly.

Wilson waved the ugly weapon under his nose. "You'll send it, all right! You'd better, if you know what's good for you!"

"Put that gun away," Turner told his partner. "These are a couple of smart kids. They know better than to try anything." His eyes narrowed to dark slits, but his voice was conciliatory and oily smooth. "You're right about that message. It is in code. But there's something you'd better remember. There's a lot of money at stake here, and we're not about to let two kids stop us."

"You're wasting time, Turner!" Wilson growled. "Let me handle 'em! That message'll be sent, and there won't be any fooling around about it!"

"What'll you do?" Turner demanded irritably. "Handle it like you handled that airplane?"

"You've been bellyachin' about that ever since I did it," Wilson snarled, "but those 'Narcs' who were in it haven't caused us any more trouble, have they? We ain't in the slammer like we would've been if I hadn't taken a hand."

"We ain't done yet."

"But we will be after Wednesday night. Once we get all that 'bread' in our greasy little mitts, we'll be long gone. Nobody'll be able to find us, so it won't make any difference about the plane crash or these kids, either."

"We don't have to get rough with the boys, Wilson," Turner said, grinning. "They're our partners."

His companion's eyes widened. "Partners? You've got to be kidding!"

"Don't you remember what the law says? If any-one helps a criminal in any way, he's guilty too. And we all know that these boys have been helping us."

Matt Barton winced.

"In fact, if I've got it right, Matthew was involved in a little incident of breaking and entering back in Colorado. Getting caught in a scheme like this would go hard with him. Don't you think?"

"How'd you know about that?" Matt demanded.

"A friend of your old man's was telling me. That's how we got the idea of coming up here in the first place. It's a nice, quiet, sparsely populated area. Just the sort of spot we need to transact our business."

"I'd never thought of that!" Wilson said. "If we get caught, these two go in the slammer with us. That's neat, Turner!"

"You know we weren't told anything about that message being in code," Matt persisted. "You said it was to be a joke on your friend. We'll tell the cops that."

"And do you think *they'll* believe you when there's all this evidence? You're the ones who stole that pot from us. Remember? That'll go hard with you, too."

"No way!" Danny retorted firmly. "We didn't steal anything from you or anyone else."

"We know better, don't we, Wilson?"

"Right on! And I wouldn't even be surprised if the 'Narcs' would be able to find some grass right here in the house."

"The Fuzz won't be up here at Angle Inlet, Minnesota. How could they find any pot here?"

Suspicion gleamed in Wilson's features.

"What'd you say that for?" he demanded.

"Why did I say what?" Matt asked.

"That part about Angle Inlet, Minnesota. Why'd you say it?"

"That's where we are, isn't it?"

"Don't talk that way to our partners," Turner said. "We've got to get that message to our friend. So, Matt, turn around and send it. OK?"

Matt did as he was told. He hoped the fellow from Minneapolis who relayed the message to their associate was off the air, but he answered immediately, as though he had been waiting for Matt to contact him. He repeated the message three times, said he would get it to the one it was intended for, and signed off.

Matt looked up. "Now that I've sent your message," he said icily, "why don't you leave?"

"Leave?" Turner echoed. "What kind of a partner are you, anyway? You can't be serious about turning us out in the cold."

"That's right," Wilson broke in. "This'll be a nice, comfortable place to wait for Wednesday night."

"And in the meantime, we'll take the boys down to the main floor and lock them in a room," Turner said, "just in case they get the idea they want to take off before we're ready to be rid of them."

"You'll have to let us go to school in the morning," Matt said. "If we aren't there, Mrs. Edgren will check on us, and Danny's dad'll be over to see why we weren't there."

"In that case," Wilson said, tapping the automatic pistol significantly, "it will be too bad for old man Orlis! We're into this deal too deep to stop now. No matter *what* we have to do!"

"Come on, you guys," Turner said. "We can't hang around up here all night."

Matt reached over to switch off the radio. The dope smuggler's cheeks blanched.

"No, you don't!" His hand snaked out and grasped Matt's wrist. "That mike's live, ain't it?"

The boy eyed him defiantly but said nothing.

"Ain't it?"

"Right on!" he said loudly. "You've just broadcasted everything you've done or planned to do to every ham operator in America who's tuned to this frequency!"

"You sneaky little brat!" He hit Matt with a mighty sweep of his open hand, knocking him sprawling. The boy hit his head against the wall and lay still, stunned momentarily. He could hear what was being said, but the voices sounded far away and indistinct.

"Get that thing shut off!" Wilson cried, groping desperately for the switch. "I *knew* something was up when he kept mentioning Angle Inlet!"

"Somebody's probably on the way over here right now," Danny said. "They'll be here any minute!"

"Don't give us that!" Turner retorted. "We know better! There ain't another ham radio up here."

"Don't fool yourself," Danny said boldly. "There's a radio at Penasse and at both Oak and Flag Islands. There are ways of getting word up here, all right. This radio just happens to be the closest to Angle Inlet, that's all."

Wilson wasn't listening. He searched frantically for the switch to turn off the radio. When he couldn't find it, he reached under the desk and jerked the cord from the electrical outlet.

"There!" he exclaimed, swearing angrily. "I've got it turned off! Now to take care of these blasted kids!"

"Are you out of your skull?" Turner demanded. "Everybody knows by now that we're here! If we do anything to these two, they'll have us before we're a hundred miles away."

"What're we goin' to do?" Wilson demanded plaintively.

"Shut up and let me think!"

Matt's head had cleared by this time. He got slowly to his feet.

"We can take the kids with us!" Wilson suggested in desperation. "As long as we've got 'em, nobody'll *dare* to take us!"

"The best shot we've got is to get on that snowmobile of ours and get out of here," Turner said, "before anyone shows up!"

"I told you we should've taken care of them brats as soon as the message was sent," Wilson retorted. "But no! You knew a *better* way!"

"Shut your mouth and let's get moving!" He grabbed Danny and Matt by the arms and shoved them down the stairs ahead of him. "Now, you two! Get your parkas and boots on and be quick about it!"

"We goin' to take 'em along?" Wilson wanted to know.

"That's the only good idea you've had!" He turned to the boys. "Now, snap it up, or I'll turn Wilson loose on you!"

The boys did as they were told. Turner jerked them to their feet and pushed them out the kitchen door. As they stepped out into the frigid arctic wind, Danny wrenched free and jumped off the porch, dashing into the darkness.

"Come back here!" Turner shouted. He lunged for the boy who had escaped his grasp. At the same instant, Matt tore himself free and leaped the other way. Turner tried to reach for him, too, but lost his balance and sprawled in the snow.

"Come back here!" Wilson shouted to the wind. "Come back or I'll shoot!"

He pulled the gun from the holster and fired it into the air. But Danny and Matt didn't stop. They ran around the corner of the house in the darkness and hid in the bush at opposite sides of the clearing. The yard light at the neighboring Erickson place switched on, flooding the drifts with a harsh, yellow light. The circle of light reached halfway to the Fuller place, casting shadows from each clump of brush, but the back door of Matt's grandma's was still shrouded in darkness.

"What's goin' on out here?" Mr. Erickson demanded loudly.

Danny and Matt both saw the light and started toward it. In the darkness Wilson cursed angrily.

"Watch out, Mr. Erickson!" Danny shouted. "They've got a gun!"

"So've I!" He dashed out of the circle of light so he wouldn't make a good target. "I'm comin', Danny! Hang in there!"

"Wilson!" Turner shrieked. "Let's get out of here while we're ahead!"

The boys heard the two men running through the snow in the direction of their snowmobile.

"Danny! Matthew!" Mr. Erickson shouted once more. "Are you boys all right?"

They both stumbled through the deep drifts to the neighbor's house.

"Aren't we going to stop them?" Matt asked.

"No need to," Erickson said, as they heard the snowmobile snarling across the frozen lake. "They'll leave a perfect trail for the sheriff to follow. Let's go into your grandma's house and radio him!"

They sent a message to the sheriff, but word came back that he was already on his way to Angle Inlet with the federal narcotics agents. Mrs. Erickson insisted that the boys stay with them that night.

They were in bed but hadn't gone to sleep at midnight when Carl Orlis, the sheriff, and the two agents who had talked to Danny and Matt at school came to the house.

"That was smart thinking, Matt," one of the narcotics officers said, "leaving the mike open on your radio and getting those guys to talking. We must've had fifty phone calls from all over the country telling us what was going on up here."

"Only getting caught at it wasn't so smart," Matt said. "If it hadn't been for that, you'd have nabbed Wilson and Turner."

"We'll get them. Don't worry about that. We've got men watching the lake at every settlement and town around it on both sides of the border. And if they try to get away into the bush, we can track them by helicopter as soon as it's daylight."

The boys both sighed their relief.

"And now," the agent went on, "with the evidence from the ham operators added to everything else we have, we should be able to break this entire dope ring—all because of you two."

The next morning Matt had his radio on when word came in that Turner and Wilson had been caught by the OPP near Kenora, Ontario, with six kilos of cocaine in their possession. The rest of the gang was also caught.

"I guess that takes care of them," Danny said.

On the way home from school that afternoon, the boys stopped again at the Orlis home.

"Your grandma's here, Matt," Danny's mom said. "She just came in by plane. She heard on the radio what happened to you and Danny and got worried."

"We were able to take care of ourselves," he muttered.

On the porch, Danny stopped and turned to Matt. "Are you going to tell her?" he asked quietly.

"About what?"

"You know."

"About my being a Christian?"

Danny nodded.

"I've got to tell her. And I've got something else to tell her, too. I decided on it last night."

"What's that?"

"I'm going back to Colorado and live with Mom. Maybe I can help her to become a Christian, too."

Danny grinned and tapped his friend on the chest with his fist.

THE
DANNY ORLIS
SERIES

The Danny Orlis series, by Bernard Palmer, delivers a blend of adventure, mystery, and suspense through various settings—from the Canadian wilderness to Guatemalan jungles. Danny Orlis, an adept outdoorsman, skilled athlete, and committed Christian, employs his quick thinking, calm bravery, and biblical solutions to confront everyday problems and hair-raising dangers. Early stories focus on Danny navigating school life, sports, and outdoor challenges, while in later books, Danny and his wife Kay provide wisdom and guidance to youngsters facing lifelike situations and challenges. Having sold over two million copies, this series has made Palmer a renowned author in Christian youth literature. Palmer is also the author of the Felicia Cartright series and various other series for Christian youth.

AVAILABLE FROM WWW.ANEKOPRESS.COM

www.ingramcontent.com/pod-product-compliance
Lightning Source LLC
Chambersburg PA
CBHW070657100726
47907CB00007B/2241